At Crossroads

At Crossroads

Fragmented Tale of Nora

Nivedita Sahoo

PARTRIDGE
A Penguin Random House Company

To order additional copies of this book, contact
Partridge India
000 800 10062 62
orders.india@partridgepublishing.com

www.partridgepublishing.com/india

This story revolves around two main characters, Nora and Bee, best of friends, who work together, shop and party together, travel and do a list of other things together.

Being with each other made life easier for both of them as they were never aware of what was there that life had to offer.

Yes dear, life is full of surprises, isn't it?

Life takes an interesting turn when Nora falls in love with a guy, that turns out to be a miserable experience and Bee had to fight against her marriage arranged by her parents, which she never planned for, rather never had it in her list.

As Nora & Bee move ahead, dealing with the changes and re-prioritizing things, they get to explore new people, different places, varied thoughts and many more.

Few chunks from this story depicts various phase, starting from the ones where "life is beautiful" to those ones where "nothing falls into place".

But may the choices be right or wrong, the fact remains the same "life never stops, neither does time, nor do we".

Chapter 1

Ring…. Ring…Ring.

Ohh, this shitty alarm!

No. It's not the alarm, seems to be my phone. Now who the hell calls me in the middle of the night?

I picked up the call without daring to open my eyes. "Hello".

"Good morning Nora."

"Oh come on Bee, you can't be serious"

Bee: "I am. It's already 8.30 a.m.; get the hell out of the bed and rush now. You don't have much of time & yeah, the meeting starts at 9.00"

Before I could say something, all I could hear was Beep. Beep.

I opened my eyes and looked for my Mobile to check if it was really half past eight in the morning. Well it was. I found a few messages and missed calls to go through. There were 5 texts, 3 WhatsApp messages, 16 FB notifications, &

6 new mails and two missed calls- one from Dad and the other one from a customer care guy.

As soon as I decided to call up dad, my phone started ringing. The call was from Dad.

"Good morning dear, get up, get ready, have your breakfast and rush to office. You are already late," he said.

That call from dad happened to be my usual wake up alarm every morning. Though not so appreciable in weekends, somehow those wakeup calls not only replenish me with renewed energy but act as a stress reliever at least for the working days.

After those expected calls, I finally left my bed and rushed to the bathroom. I was happily having my shower not realizing I was already late when a phone call again from Bee woke me up to reality.

'Where the hell are you? It is 8.55', she shouted.

Believe me, when I heard her, I literally felt I would be a Dead meat that day.

'Yes, I would be right there within 15...' I replied with a shaky voice.

'Fifteen minutes. You are kidding me, right Nora?'

'Ok. I am almost there. Give me five minutes?'

'Cool. Come soon.' Bee hung up and I ran towards my wardrobe to pick anything, just anything to put on and leave for office.

Then a look on the checklist stuck at the door, Mobile-taken, mob charger- taken, purse, laptop, laptop charger-taken, ID card- done, scooter keys- taken, Door Lock- Close the door and, Done. I rushed down stairs, brought my scooter from the parking and moved.

Well the scooter has a history too- It could ditch you anytime. She is as moody as I am. But luckily it started that day.

The journey towards the office started. The traffic, as always looked heavy and I being the expert driver had to manage myself through the gaps and corners without hitting anyone. Anyway I was sure that I won't be reaching on time. The road seemed like a long one but finally it ended. I quickly parked the scooter, locked it and started walking at a flying speed trying to make it to my cubicle. When I reached there, I saw no one around, and that meant they were in the meeting room. The meeting was scheduled to start at 9.00 a.m. and I was 20 minutes late. Disaster for sure!!

First thing that came to mind was to open my laptop, then Microsoft outlook and check the Meeting request to find out about the meeting room. When I opened my mailbox, I saw a mail stating that the meeting was cancelled. Oh such a relief it was!

And about my colleagues, I was sure they would be busy with some other stuff or hanging by the cafeteria. I wanted to meet Bee but she was nowhere there in the office. 'Chuck it Nora! She would rather find me if necessary.' As I was still sleepy I thought of having a cup of coffee. When I walked through the cafeteria to get my cup, I saw Bee sitting there with Daniel Drake, looked like they were having their usual one on one conversation.

Daniel Drake, the Manager of the team, was the self-proclaimed Mr. Right whom every one feared but no one respected.

I saw Bee explaining something to him as he shook his head with a to and fro motion at such a speed that for a while I felt his head would break off his body and come rolling near me. I very well knew he was going to make Bee's day miserable. Well… I didn't have to do much but just to be mentally prepared and face the heat.

I quickly grabbed a glass of milk, didn't go for coffee and rushed back to office.

As I turned around to walk to my cubicle I clashed with somebody, and yes, he was none other than Harry with a smile. 'Hello Nora, are you upset with me, you literally broke my fingers.'

'And what the hell were you doing behind me?'

"Oh! I was trying to scare you. That happened the other way. Well.. This was even cool…I guess…" Harry said.

"Come on Harry. That wasn't, and listen customers come back saying they need a fix. So loads of things to discuss and work on."

Harry said in his sarcastic tone-"Wonderful news, I am thinking of taking a week's break. Else I am sure I would fall sick because of these shitty customers. Hahaha.."

I was sure that day was going to be a long and hectic one. We had few meetings, two of them late in the evening. Few of our senior colleagues work from U.S and we have to sync up with them, which means late evening meet for us.

I started work by replying to the mails and I was going through one of them when I saw Bee coming back to her seat. I thought I would ping her later but Bee always did the honor. I saw a pop-up in the bottom right of my screen that said:

Bee: (C)

I knew what it meant. I opened the chat window and saw a coffee mug. That is how she calls me for a break.

I just had my milk but I knew this shouldn't be an excuse and I would have to accompany her. That symbol not only signifies coffee but also "we need to talk".

Before I could reply to her, she walked up to me and locked my laptop screen. And I made my way towards cafeteria, again, and this time with Bee.

'I can never really understand what the issue is. Jerk… The process needs to be changed, I mean. Seriously!! A process that has been followed from more than 10 years needs to be changed. He knows everything because he is a qualified experienced employee.. Ha-ha..Nora.. Do you know a qualified experienced psychiatrist whom I can suggest him to? Bloody paranoid.'

'Ahh!! I understand. Take a deep breath. I hate him too. But for now let's go back as we will be having our daily meet,' I tried to console her.

The situation was under control and we were just about to go back when Angela walked in 'Hello girls; I was there speaking over the phone when I noticed you both.. Is everything fine? And Bee, why do you look as if you met Drake this morning?'

'Or. Wait; was it something by Mr. Cliff...?' She asked.

Angela and me both looked at each other and quickly turned to look at Bee. "Holy shit" that has to be something from Mr. Cliff.

'Bee, let's move else Mr. Cliff might die out of shock if he doesn't see us online,' said Angela

'Yes I am sure he would literally choke,' Bee replied.

Hahaha. Angela and I burst out laughing looking at Bee making a variety of funny faces.

Chapter 2

It was the daily meet which was the toughest part of the day. You got to speak about the updates and the daily progress and this means, if you are in office you have to work and surely you can't fake it.

As we all had an usual meeting, meanwhile Bee's group had a tough time with Daniel Drake and we were more interested to sneak a peek to theirs rather than our own. While others took 10 minutes to get over, they took 45 minutes for no specific reason. After all it was Daniel (Mr. happy for nothing) Drake and he required explanations. The soldiers started with their daily updates, each one of them took 10 minutes for their individual stand-up status update. Once Daniel was satisfied with the fact that his team would really be working for the day, he would let them go.

That day they did it for 40 minutes and after a long Q and A session, finally they were done.

I saw a ping in my messenger as soon as Bee was back to her seat,

Bee- I hate doing this.

'Doing what?'

Bee- To work for this guy.

Nora- Ahh!! Chill baby…what happened?

Bee- Nothing new. He again forgot my update and I had to remind him that I was done with the documentation.

Nora- Ok. Don't worry. You must be used to it by this time.

Bee- Yeah. Big time.

Nora-- Chill. Will speak over the lunch.

Bee- Cool.

It was exact 12.00 pm when all the girls in the team gather for lunch.

Bee, Angela and I had a different preference for lunch. We hated the team accompanying us for lunch as that was our own time. Because that is the time where we used to share and discuss all kind of topics that include personal, professional matters in which we can't involve anyone else. That was another reason for three of us being good friends.

That day was a team lunch day. There was no specific reason – but just to remind ourselves that we are not yet out of the Team. After all end of the day we had to work as a Team.

We all gathered at the lift lobby, took the lift to 6th floor. That's where we used to have our lunch.

We had Veronica, Ashley, Mary, Bee, I, Angela & Jonna joining us that day.

Let me tell you, this was a real interesting group. All of us walked up to the buffet to collect our food. We had different variety and I almost collected bit of everything. We took a bench and started taking our lunch. This group always had things to chat on during lunch time and that day the topic was "outing".

'What about the team outing guys?' Bee asked.

Angela said looking at me & Bee "I think it would never happen".

She turned towards Ashley, "Ashley. Any Updates?"

Ashley was asked because she once mentioned that she would speak to Mr. Cliff about this.

"Yes. I mean I would speak to him if you guys want me too", said Ashley

Veronica added, "we would love to if you can do this for us."

Jonna- Well. Well good luck for that. I am sure you are going to crack it this time.

To tell you, that was the 3rd effort Ashley had put on for the Team outing.

The post lunch part was usually very lazy, with a couple of meeting where we had to manage keeping our eyes open. Definitely the power nap of 10 minutes post lunch helped. Well, thanks to the person who invented it.

After a long tiring afternoon, finally it was 5.00 pm. Time to return home.

Very quickly I packed my bag and called Bee.

Bee- Did you get your scooter Nora?

Yes I did. Let's zooommmmmm.

Bee- Hahaha. Don't give me that shit. Your bike hardly moves.

'Say whatever!!! I reply with an annoyed look…And we move.

Chapter 3

As we reached the parking lot I saw the scooter parked with its double stand, and till date I have never learnt the art of pulling it off its stand. So the only option was to call the guard again.

Hey there. Excuse me. Sir!! Can you please get my scooter off those stands? Please? I called up for the guard.

Sir!! Didn't I tell you people not to put those middle stands for my scooter and let it be as I leave it?

Bee murmurs looking at me- Crazy Lady!!!

"Bee, did you just say Crazy?"

No ways. Never, she replies.

Ok anyway. Doesn't matter.

Meanwhile the scooter was off its stand. I thanked the guard and he left commenting "mam, you should eat more to get the scooter off those middle stands." I know that was offending.

We stayed nearby. Bee's place was some 700 meters from mine. It was the same layout.

I stayed alone and Bee with her roomie Clarke, Benny Clarke.

Staying near helped us getting the entire daily jobs done easily, starting from grocery shopping, to having a coffee or having an unexpected trip together.

'Nora. I am hungry. Let's have a coffee and eat something before we go back home,' Bee said.

'Coffee day then?'

'Yea sure,' Bee replied.

We stopped by the nearest Coffee Day Lounge. And I parked my scooter by the road side.

"Oh come on. You can park it anywhere. Anyway no one would like to take this outdated stuff of yours," Bee said.

Cool. I have nothing to say, let's go have Coffee.

We took our favorite corner and ordered for coffee. The waiter came back with our order in a while and we started sipping our coffee accompanied by all sorts of discussions.

As we believe, all good ideas come over a coffee, but for our ideas…that is completely a different story.

Bee said while taking her coffee,' It's been a long time we had a vacation. Let's plan for one. What about Goa to end this week with?'

Goa is a place that we both used to visit almost every 6 months for the last 3 years. It felt like a home away from home and a place, where we can breathe deep, walk fast and let go all our day to day frustration.

And being a travel freak, to listen something like this was always a pleasure. "Sure, we can skip a workday; I think that shouldn't be an issue".

'Skipping a day? Nora you remember Mr. Cliff right? Do you want to get surprises in your inbox?' Bee reminded me.

"Arrgghhh… As if we care" I said.

'Yeah that we don't. So Thursday it is. You look for a Hotel and I book the tickets. Deal done.'

So once we were done with the plan over the coffee, we got back home.

Both of us weren't that happy to be at office the next day, we had a holiday plan lined up for the weekend, now who wants to stay back in office.

It was all about attending the meetings with a lousy mood, and somehow getting the pending job done so that no one bothers us on our holiday.

The plan was to leave Bangalore on Thursday after office hour and get back by Sunday. Tickets were reserved, hotel was booked and the only thing that was left was to make up an excuse for not attending the office on Friday.

Chapter 4

We jumped off the taxi hanging around few bags by our shoulders and started running towards the bus. We were late, because of Bee's idea of having a lavish dinner before boarding the bus.

We both went in different directions to search the "Bangalore to Goa" bus. After running around for some time I found the bus. "There it is" I shouted - feeling proud of unwinding a mystery. I called up Bee to let her know. "yes I heard you, and so did everyone else" she said. Be there, I am coming". She took out the tickets and showed it to the conductor asking if that was the same bus.

'Yes mam. This is the one. Board the Bus. We are about to leave. No water and toilet now, directly at the next stop' the conductor replied.

We dumped our bags in the bus carrier and took our seats, or beds we can say. That was an upper berth but it seemed to be a comfortable one. They had a white bed sheet that covered the leather seats, 2 pillows and a blanket and to my surprise those were clean. They also had curtains to cover the berth. This was not the first time we travelled by bus but we were travelling by a sleeper bus for the first time.

The bus started towards Goa and I almost skipped a beat. That was excitement. I was super excited thinking about where we would be when we get up tomorrow morning. I wanted to lie down and close my eyes as soon as I could. But I was sure that is not going to happen till Bee was with me.

'Nora, Beer?' Bee said.

'Yeah cool,' I said holding up the can and cheers.

Though drinking was strictly prohibited in the bus, still we managed to enjoy couple of Beer as we had those curtains to cover us.

After having few gulps, Bee suddenly turned towards me. I looked at her when she gave me a confusing look.

What happened? I asked

"Nora, are you sure they are going to stop somewhere for a while?

'Well. I am not sure about it, but why? Do you need something?'

Yes, I need to spill this Beer out of my body. In short I need to pee, Bee said.

That was the moment when I realized that I too have almost emptied a can of Beer and I would also require getting that out. I said consoling her,' I think so, I mean I hope so. Let's wait, that's what we can do for now.'

And we continued looking out of the glass window. It was dark but I could still see the moon peeping through the clouds, and the trees appeared running back at furious speed. I kept staring at the moon for a while and then I closed my eyes.

Suddenly I heard someone tapping on our seat. I got up with a heavy head and I saw a man peeping through the curtains.

'Who are you and what are you looking at?' I asked

'Madam, it's a 15 minutes stop. If you want to go and freshen up or have something to eat or drink, you can. But just 15 minutes you got.'

He was the conductor.

'Jesus. You just scared me to death.'

'Bee was still sleeping. Bee, bee, wake up. It's just a 15 minutes stop, bee.'

'Yes, Yes. Where are we? What happened? Are we safe? Are you fine?' She woke up getting shocked.

'Arggg…Nothing happened, It's a 15 minutes stop. Now get down.'

That was 12.30 am, the place was somewhere in the middle of nowhere. There was a small food center. There were few shops too, but they were closed. There were no proper toilets but they had those temporary cabins built where you could go, get freshen up and pay for that.

The first thing we had to do was to walk towards the toilet. There was a guy standing outside the toilets who says, Mam, its 10 rupees, 5 rupees for each of you.

Bee took 10 rupee out of her pocket handed it over to the man.

As we entered the cabin, yuucckkkkk…Those were stinking. There was no water supply, no lights. There was a water tank with no water in it, plus it was dirty, very dirty. Anyway we were not left with much of options, so we had to choose the one we had. Thanks to the torch app installed in our mobile.

Bee was literally flushed looking at the place, and I was sure the person who charged 10 bucks for letting us pee in that monument of his, was into a big trouble.

'Shame on you' Bee shouted at the person. 'Ten rupees for this shitty toilet, you got to be kidding me. Get my money back you moron. I am not gonna pay you even a single buck for this.'

'No madam, you used the toilet so you'll have to pay.'

'And pay for what?' Bee asked.

'For maintenance of the toilets,' said the guy.

'Bee with her surprised look, what?? Did you say maintenance? Nora, did he just say, he charged us for the maintenance of those toilets? Hahaha…Are you on drugs or something? Get my money back you jerk else I am gonna make a scene out here.'

'Madam, you cannot use toilets without paying', he said and gave us back the 10 rupee note with a grinning look that was complimentary. Well I would say, looking at Bee, any person with self-respect would have returned the money.

There was a tea corner attached to the food center.

'Bee, let's go have some tea.'

'Yes lets go, but if the tea is for 10 rupee, I am not going to have it for sure,' replied Bee

'Hahaha. Cool lets go.'

'Sir, two cups of tea please,' I asked.

'Madam, that's 20 rupee,' and I looked at Bee.

Before Bee could spill out something, I paid him 20 bucks.

Bee looked at me as if I had murdered someone and asked her to take the blame.

'Bee, chill. Have some tea, you would feel better plus this tastes nice. Being irritated on someone really doesn't worth missing this.'

'Hmmmm Ok, if you say so. Anyway you have already paid him. She picked up the paper cup and took a few sips.'

I searched my mobile to check if anyone has called. Anyone means either dad or mom because I never take any other call at night. It has to be mom or dad or…Bee whom I would speak if I feel like speaking. For that reason, I had a long list of missed calls in the call records.

I checked the mobile, No missed calls. Thank god. I hate lying. Yes, Mom and dad were not aware of the plan.

Meanwhile the conductor started screaming that he was about to leave. We rushed towards the bus and pushed us inside through the door.

Chapter 5

Nora, get up, we reached Margao. Not too far now-Bee said waking me up. I slowly opened my eyes and looked through the glass window. The weather was beautiful. It looked sunny but not hot. That was the month of November, so the sun wasn't that mean to us and that's why I think I preferred this place all over again.

After a while we started packing up our stuffs and got ourselves a ready so that we don't look like aliens by the time we reach.

Within minutes we reached Panaji bus stop. Though Panaji is a popular tourist spot and most of the travelers prefer staying there, we never liked staying at Panaji, perhaps because of the heavy crowd. We had to take a cab for our destination. Bike was a better choice but we were too tired after a long journey to ride 35 to 40kms.

There were a number of taxis lined up.' Madam, looking for a taxi?' A guy out from the crowd asked.

'Yes, to Arambol. How much?' I enquired.

'Seven hundred rupees,' the cab driver said.

"That is too much. This is not the first time we are visiting Goa. Make it 500 and we go."

"Madam, not possible. Pay me 600."

"Ok. 550. that is final." And we dumped our bags and ourselves in the back seat.

We had an overnight journey, and so were tired, yet, I loved the drive from Panaji to Arambol. I somehow loved to see the people moving around in bikes, cars, jeeps, loved those roadside shops, those hanging colorful dresses and other flea stuff, the salty breeze hitting our faces, those coconut groves as if they are following the roads we were driving through, and in fact everything seemed to be like Gods one of the best creations.

We headed towards the extreme north of Goa, crossing Anjuna, Mapusa, Siolim and few other places. We enjoyed the journey, while the driver was busy explaining about the on & off seasons in Goa, the flea markets, parties and what not.

The place where we were heading to is basically a village. It is a kind of a secluded spot and that is why we would see fewer travelers, and mostly foreigners.

We left the cab 2 km away from where we were supposed to stay. We had a shack booked by the beach side, and the cab wasn't allowed to go near the beach because of the narrow street and the market covering the road from both the sides. We walked down the streets crossing different shops, few restaurants, tour & travel centers, guest houses, handicrafts, tattoo studios and many more. Everything around looked so colorful, I can say, it looked like an artifact and accessories exhibition. I used to get so fascinated whenever I came here. It was indeed a nice place to spend time quietly without any outside interference.

Once we reached the beach we started walking towards the left, crossing the beach side shack restaurants.

It was a bit away from the entrance of the beach and took almost 20 to 25 minutes on foot. On the way we noticed how beautifully they had maintained the restaurants (they were all shacks). They never build a permanent one, because those would be just open in the tourist season, and during the off season as there would be no or very few travelers they would close it. I was so lost in sightseeing that I never realized when we reached our destination.

Bee looked exhausted. She rushed in to the reception and said to the long haired guy standing there. "Hey, we booked for a shack. This is the booking confirmation. Can you please help us?"

"Sure mam. Please give me a minute". He checked the sheet, found out a vacant shack for us and led us to that. We were lucky enough because the shack was situated in an amazing location. It was towards east, facing the sea and the sea line was so near that you can enjoy the view if you sit in the portico of the shack. It was a clean room. There was a bedroom, attached bathroom, one table, few chairs, and a kitchen in there and a table fan. It almost looked like a hippie's den, but we liked it.

'Yaaaayaaa. Nora, we are in Goa. Yes. We are back. We are gona rock the floor.' Bee shouted entering our room. That's when I realized she was even as excited as I was.

Chapter 6

'Nora, do you see this? Its 11.00 am and we have not had any food. I think we should go and have something to eat,'said Bee.

"Yes. I am ready, let's go."

In fact, there was no food service for those shacks. We had to walk down the beach towards the main entrance to find restaurants which we crossed while walking in. There were many but we went for the one named as Buddha palace. The name seemed decent and the crew was local people and looked like a nice place to hang out.

We entered the place and occupied two chairs facing the sea. The walls had colorful designs. And most of the people around us, in the restaurant, were blacks. For the very first time I looked around, believe me, I thought it was a Jamaican restaurant but in reality that was a local hub.

The waiter arrived with a menu card, placed it on our table.

Bee said, without even having a look in the menu. "Yes, get us two beers, and the best starter made with mushrooms. We would order for the main course few minutes later."

Because of Bee being a foodie and her choice for delicacies, whenever it was about food, I used to go by Bee's choice.

The waiter opened the beer bottles and placed the plate of stuffed mushroom.

'Cheers to our friendship,' Bee said.

'Cheers to the togetherness,' I exclaimed and began taking our drinks.

We were enjoying our drink when I noticed a guy walking towards us. He looked attractive but messy- looked as if he had not made his hair for days. He was shirtless, hanging a blue cloth with Om prints all over it, around his shoulders. Seemed like he loved flaunting.

(Well, why won't he. He has a perfectly structured body, nothing much or nothing less).

I was very much confident about the people I see at this place because I used to be a regular visitor. Because of my earlier visits I could find many familiar faces and even had a few local friends.

"Might be his first visit. I have never seen this guy before," I said.

"Neither did I," said Bee agreeing with me.

He passed by and went towards the counter while I kept an eye on him when he ordered his drink.

I wanted to remain indifferent to him and enjoy my drink and the surrounding. But believe me; it was very difficult to keep my eyes off him. I continued enjoying my

Beer and staring towards the sea for a few seconds and…not for long, I turned around, damn it, even he was looking at me. Yes, it was our first eye to eye contact. We kept looking at each other for a second or so when the waiter brought him his drink.

I quickly came back to my senses but then again compulsively I wanted to have a glance of the young man; unfortunately he was gone by then. I saw him walking in the sea beach. 'Does he stay here? And where is he going? I thought.' Goodness me, why should I be anyhow bothered about where the hell he goes.

Nora, do you hear me. Nora!!

'Shit man' in a whispering tone.. Yupp Bee, tell me.

"Where were you? I have been speaking to you for five minutes and did you get anything of what I said?" Bee asked with a frustrated tone.

'Yes, something' I said. (Trust me I didn't even listen to a single word of what she was saying.)

'Okay Bee. Leave it, would you like to accompany me for a walk towards the cliff?'

'Certainly we will, but after we have our lunch.'

'Cool.

As per Bee's terms, wherever we are or whatever we would be doing doesn't matter till we are having the meals in time. We took our lunch and started walking towards the cliff.

"So what do we have there?" Bee asked as we walked towards the cliff.

"Ahh. Nothing much but a few shops, restaurants and a lake", I replied

'A lake, by a beach? That's weird.'

"Yes, we have a lake nearby and trust me it looks beautiful."

Those cliffs were just near the beach. The way to the cliff was exquisite, a place where you would love taking a walk.

The road followed the sea. Both sides of the lane were decorated with shops hanging colorful merchandise all over. There were restaurants, books stalls, music stores, guest houses and many more. That was post noon and the sun made it look more beautiful.

We walked by the shops, crossing the cliffs towards the other side of the beach. There were tourists roaming around and local people working hard to attract more of them.

(Bee kept looking around and I was looking for someone who was the sole reason for the long walk after our meal. And yes I found him, finally.

"Hey how have you been?" he asked

"Yeah. I am doing great. Better than the last time. What do you have?" I asked.

"Ahhh…I have pure Manali stuff, he puts his hand in his pocket to get a pinch of it and places it in my palm."

"And this smells awesome. I said smelling it. I would like to have some."

He got a pouch from his pocket," here it is, 1000 bucks," he said.

'Cool.' I looked at Bee. She asked with disgust "Is this the reason for which you made me walk more than a kilometer?"

"Chill. Get me one thousand rupees and we would leave," I said.

She was the one who carried a purse always and I used to stuff everything in there.

She handed me a 1000 rupee note but with her nasty look.

I handed it over to the guy and we returned. I was sure once the person left I would have to face the heat and I did..

'What the hell was that Nora? You got to be kidding me, I mean, seriously?

'Yea, I mean, let's try it once. Not a big deal, Right? Well, no big deal. Honestly, I am excited too,' said Bee.

Chapter 7

The music was loud and it sounded amazing. I and Bee took the nearest possible seats to the console; they had a band playing for them that evening. We had our roll ready and were literally excited to try it out once we walked out, but the music was kind of holding us back.

The place was nice, and the overall environment made us feel relaxed and happy. We started talking about random things about office, about the place and the people and what not.

"So when are we going back?" Bee asked

"Oh, come on Bee. We just reached today. We will speak about it later."

"Cool, if you say so."

"I would be back in a minute Bee". And I walked up to the counter where I unexpectedly met the guy whom I had seen at the Buddha Palace. I was stunned into silence for a moment as our eyes clashed.

"Hi; I am Tobios." He stretched his hand towards me.

I struggled for breath for a few seconds, and then, "hey Tobias, nice to see you. I am Nora," I replied.

"Nice to see you here, Nora. And it is pronounced as Tobios. Tooo- biii-ooss. To-bi-os," He said.

"Ahh. Sorry, hey Tobios. How have you been?"

"I am doing great, so you are alone?"

"No, I am with my friend. She is over there," I replied pointing towards Bee.

"Oh great. Enjoy the party then. Will see you later Nora." He picked his drink and bade me bye and moved away.

By the time I said Bye, he had already left. I was still awe struck by what just happened and was totally confused.

"Oh my goodness, he might be the one I am looking for." I saw him moving towards the pool table. He hugged few guys hanging around the pool board, looked like, he was accompanied by his friends.

Being still in shock, I walked back to my table.

"Nora, you don't look well. Are you fine? You want some rest," Bee asked.

"No. Bee listen, I met Tobios."

"Okay, that's great. I am glad you guys met, but would you be so kind to tell me who the hell he is?"

"Ohh. Bee, the guy we met at Buddha Palace. You remember?"

"The Buddha palace guy? Yes. That messy moron?" Bee remarked.

"Come on Bee. He looks good with his messy look."

"Oh yeah, am sure he does," and she got up to do her typical Scooby bum shake dance. I too joined her after a while.

We danced till midnight then decided to return to our shack. We started walking towards the beach when I heard someone calling me; I wondered who would call me in the middle of the night. I didn't see any of my friends in the café; neither had I made any new ones, we both turned back and saw Tobios walking up to us.

"I have been searching for you in the club," he said.

Bee interrupted him not even letting him finish: "Yeah, you did? Well she missed you too, didn't you, Nora?" Her voice was a bit harsh. I had to persuade her to keep quiet for a while.

"Okay. Let me know when you guys are done," she retorted.

"Hey Tobias. Sorry I didn't hear you calling. Tell me" I asked.

"I just wanted to ask if you guys would like to join us for this party tomorrow evening, if you guys are free." And He handed me a pamphlet.

"Sure, we would try to drop in if we had no other plans for tomorrow."

"Yeah. Would love to see you guys at the party," he exclaimed with a smile.

I guess the smile was enough to convince me to go to the party.

"So, Goodnight guys have a great time," he said shaking hands with Bee.

"Goodnight Tobios".

He turned to me and when I extended my hand for the shake, he pulled me towards him for a hug. Jesus!! That was so intense; I literally got butterflies in my tummy. That felt amazing. He left, and we came back to the shack. We were so tired that we didn't take much time to pass into deep slumber.

Next day early morning, that was 7.10 a.m. when my phone started ringing. It was a call from Mom.

"Hey Mom, how have you been?"

"I am doing great Nora, but would you please tell me why your number is unreachable? I have been trying to call you since yesterday."

Mom might be some network issues.

"Since a day, isn't it?" Mom asked.

Whether I agree or not, I was sure she knew something was fishy. After all she is mom, she gets to know things.

"Yeah, I mean I am not sure about the Network."

"Forget it; tell me how have you been? Are you taking your meals properly?" Mom asked showing her concern for me.

"Yupp. I am doing great mom. Work goes fine, and I am taking my meals in time. How is dad?"

"He is fine. He was just a bit concerned about you as you were not reachable. Will ask him to call you."

"Sure mom."

"Ok then bye. Take care and be in touch."

"Bye Mom and you too take care."

After the call I was hardly able to sleep. Bee was still sleeping. I thought of not disturbing her and rather taking a walk by the beach, alone. I got up, carried my mobile, picked up the joint that I remembered we didn't try the day before that was still there in my purse, and walked towards the beach. The morning looked amazing and I was not able to take my eyes off the scenic beauty of that place.

I walked up to the water and slowly immersed my feet into it. Wow!! I felt the heaven. It was 7.30 a.m., the weather was calm & breezy and the water was cool.

The beach was not yet crowded as it was early in the morning and people usually sleep late in Goa, at least that late that they won't get up till 10.00 am. The fishermen go fishing late night and that is the time when they come back.

I sat down by the beach and started enjoying the waves which looked like dancing to and fro, with their hips moving up and down. And they looked better than Shakira.

Chapter 8

'What would it look like if there were no waves in the sea?

How do those sailors find their way out in this vast never ending water body?' Yeah, I remembered the famous poem "The ancient mariner". Those stupid questioned made me laugh at myself.

I was very much lost in my thoughts when suddenly I heard someone saying, "Would you mind if I join you?"

"Goodness me, that was "Tobios". It was an early morning surprise. Hey Tobias"- I said (The pronunciation of his name was intentional).

"Noraahhh, I am Tobios"…

"Haha. Cool, and would be my pleasure if you join me. Come sit."

"What are you up to, this early?"

"I got up early so just thought of having a walk by the beach alone."

"That's great; I believe everyone should have their lone time once in a while. Helps reaching Moksha and Self –enlightenment, he said looking straight into my eyes. "I was totally bewildered by those lofty ideals and my vacant looks explained it all.

Suddenly he started laughing and said, "I was kidding Nora. I guess you took it seriously."

"Ohh.. Yeah.".I said, taking my eyes off him.

"And what made you awake so early?" I asked.

"I get up early to have my morning bath followed by a heavy breakfast, I believe in keeping myself healthy," he replied.

"That's the secret. That's good."

"So, Nora. Are you on for the party tonight?"

"I think we would be joining you for the gig tonight, though I have not spoken to Bee about this but I hope she would feel like partying tonight."

"Yeah, I know. Parties are kind of boring now days, but rely on me for this one….," he said

"That's great and I believe you."

We kept silent for a while as we had nothing else to talk about.

Quiet obvious, we hardly knew each other and we hardly had anything in common. I thought of starting a conversation as I felt it was getting odd.

"So, where are you from, Tobias?" I asked him

"Cool…he said, I would note it as Tobias, Nora."

"Haha. Let me call you Tob. Short and sweet, so where are you from Tob?".

"Yes that sounds good. I am from France. There is a region named Burgundy, this place is mostly popular for wine. That is where I come from. And where are you from?"

"I am from Bangalore. That is some 700 kms away from Goa."

"Yea, I know where Bangalore is? Cool place."

'Have you ever been to Bangalore?'

"Yes, he said, I have few friends there. I keep visiting once in a while."

"Oh, that is amazing. So seems like you have been in India for quite a while then?"

"Yes, it's been three years in India; I keep travelling from place to place for the event stuff. Depends on the season you know."

'Event? Don't tell me you are into events?' I asked.

"Haha, that is somewhat true. I work for an entertainment group that deals in gigs, travels, events and little stuff like that, and we are known as 'Decibels'."

'Oh that sounds great. It must be fun. Decibels, huh!!'

'Well, it just sounds fun.'

'So the evening event you invited us for, is something organized by you guys?'

'Yepp. You are correct. I stay here in Goa for its peak season of four months. I come this way for a while to relax but usually prefer staying by Anjuna.'

'And that is why you seemed new to me at this place,' I asked.

'So I assume you noticed me well, Nora?'

'I did, a bit,' I said with a wink.

There is a noticeable silence again..

He pulled out the cigarette packet from his pocket and offered me one.

'No, Thanks,' I said.

He lighted one, and then I remembered I had a joint.

'Hey I have a joint. Would you..'

'You do? Awesome, light it Nora,' he exclaimed, not even letting me complete the sentence.

I lighted it up and passed it to him.

He tried it and said, 'the stuff is nice, where did you get it from?'

'From the other side I replied.'

'Ok.. I know that guy, just never tried him out, and was not aware that he gets good stuff.'

'Well, sometime he does. And you must be getting late for your bathe.'

'Yes. Why don't you join me,' he asked, and suddenly those butterflies in my tummy started jumping. But I restrained myself said,' No you carryon and I would rather be here and enjoy the breeze.'

'Hmm. Ok then join me if you feel like.' He got up, took his shirt and his slippers off and walked into the water.

Did I just say "he took off his shirt"? You know what, let me tell you this, I have seen guys without a shirt; it's not that I have never seen one, but this one guy was amazing. Those heavy shoulders, that abs may be 6 of the, the perfectly shaped love handles, though not with a shirt on but without that, he just looked like a person one would love to dream of.

Looking at him I thought was I drunk that I refused him when he asked me to come along. But I was sure about myself that I won't stick by the beach for much time. I waited till he got into the water and took few dips, and then I got up to walk towards him. I didn't have to bother much about changing, I was wearing short and a t-shirt and I could very much afford getting it wet for that guy.

He waved to me when he saw me coming and I felt flattered by the way he was looking at me. The confidence with which he extended his arm and the sweet smile lingering on his lips simply benumbed me.

I didn't remember wading through the water, but my feet just swept off automatically and soon I found myself standing in front of him, very near to him grasping his fingers with mine. That was the first time I felt him so close. His eyes were into mine. His face had very sharp features, a stunningly straight nose, perfectly shaped lips and a beautiful chin. Moreover he looked irresistible, I bowed to move a step ahead and he pulled me near and bent a bit towards me. I knew what was coming, yes that was our first kiss; beneath the open sky and the wide spread sea around our feet. Hell yeahhhh. It couldn't have been more romantic than this. That moment looked so perfect to me; I just wished I was on the other side of the picture.

We stopped right there knowing well the implications and we were matured enough. We enjoyed a few dips in the water and played with the waves together for a while and I decided to go back as Bee might be looking for me because I knew if she didn't find me there, she would create a scene.

"I think I should move now, and will see you later in the evening," I said.

"Sure, be there for the gig, bye."

I gave him a hug, waved him bye and started running towards the shack.

Chapter 9

That was 9.55 p.m. when we reached the place. The party had just started so the place wasn't that crowded. It was a club house, located at Anjuna beach. We entered the club and walked towards the bar counter. I saw Tobios leaning at the counter. I was somehow very excited to see him, but at the same time Bee was not. The truth is Bee never wanted to come for the party; in fact she wanted to lazy around at the beach, so she didn't look that happy to be there.

'Hey Nora. Hey Bee, how have you been?'

'I am great, thank you, how is it going here?' Bee replied with a boring smile.'

'Yes, it goes well till now and expecting it to be good. But really nice to see you guys here. Bee, don't you worry, am sure you are going to love it.'

You wonder how he knew about her mood. Well!! She had that grumpy face carrying with her all over around portraying the torture she faced coming with me for the party.

'Yes, I think so; let's go get something to drink and a place to dump our ass' Bee said, and we walked up to the bar. I was happy to see that Tobios also joined us and I already had butterflies dancing ring-a- roses inside my tummy.

I tried starting a conversation to make up Bees mood. 'Bee, you know Tob is from France and…he loves wine.'

Tobios looked at me surprisingly when I winked at him.

'Wow, great to hear that, France is a beautiful place, isn't it?' Bee asked.

'Yes it is. France is beautiful' Tobios replied.

We were just having a casual conversation when a guy walked up to us; he patted Tobios and asked, "hey Tobi, how are you? Into the blues?"

'Hey Joy. How are you, all well?'

'Yea, I am good. This place seems rocking, killah music and this is fun.'

'Sure. Cheers Joy. Oh sorry, let me introduce you. She is Bee and she is Nora and this guys here is Joy,' Tob said gesturing towards us.

'Nice meeting you guys. So, bro see you in a while then,' said Joy and walked away.

The place was heating up; there were a number of party poppers coming in. The best thing about the club was that it was situated on the beach and there were options for other shacks lined up by the beach so probably if we don't like it here, we can just walk up to another one for a change.

The music was good, the place was rocking but who cares, I was just concentrating on Tobios. The way he was, the way he met people and greeted them, his gestures, the way he behaved, everything somehow amazed me.

'So Tobi Huh? And you seem to have a lot of friends here in Goa,' I asked.

'Yes, I have friends all over India,' he said flaunting his smile. I am sure he knows that he has got a beautiful smile but that doesn't mean he keeps showing it off. No doubt he has a lot of friends, I thought.

'Cool, Bee, Nora you guys enjoy, I got to meet my friends, would be away for a while, Hope you won't mind?'

'Oh no, sure, you carry on, we are OK,' I assured.

He walked away, letting us have our own time. I actually never wanted it at that time; rather I would have loved, if he stayed with me.

I turned towards Bee to chit chat.' I know you are not very happy with this whole party plan, sorry to drag you here. Let me know if you feel like going back, we would leave.'

'Come on Nora its fine. I would have told you if this wouldn't have interested me. This isn't even that bad. I kind of like it, but I am just confused with this "Tobios- Nora" thing. I mean everything else looks fine. Speaking to Tobios fine, coming for the party, fine, but coming for a party without even enquiring about the music and Artists, that is not something you usually do.'

'Well!! Bee, there is nothing like what you are suspecting it to be. It is just a liking for each other, may be.'

'Yes I get that Nora,' Bee remarked with a naughty smile.

'Ohh!! Please, don't give me that look, I said, but then, yes, I somehow liked Bee saying me that.' I kind of blushed.

'And you stop giving me that "Nothing like that" attitude and she started singing One love "One Love! One Heart, Let's get together and feel all right".

I was speaking to Bee, but I could still feel Tobios around. I gulped down another beer just to avoid thinking about him, but wasn't able to get him out of my mind, not even for a moment. I was not feeling well, but I didn't want to leave the place right then. At that time I noticed Tob walking towards us with another Man with dreadlocked hair and literally dressed in rags. He looked to be a local.

'Hey girls, this is Troy, Troy they are Nora and Bee. He is a close friend and also one of the partners in Crime, we work together.'

'Hey Troy, how are you?' I wished.

'I am doing great, Thank you and good to see you here.'

I was hoping Bee to wish him or at least smile at him, but she asked,' are those dreadlocks real?'

'Yes, those are for real,' he replied.

'Yeah, let me compliment you then, those actually look amazingly crazy on you,' Bee said. Finally Bee looked a bit cheerful and good.

'They do? Well thank you.'

Tob and I were having a thought on doing few events in Bangalore because the place has got a huge party crowd.

'It's great to know that you have considered Bangalore and yes we got a lot of party people there. I am sure you will not regret the decision of organizing an event there provided you do proper marketing before the event,' I said.

It took me a lot to convince him, and now Tob would have to convince other members (Matt and Will) of the 'Decibels for the purpose.

'I don't see them around Troy, where are they?' Tob asked.

'Not sure, but if not here then I think they would be at the beach smoking shit out there. Forget them, so for how many days you guys are here for?'

'Oh, we are here for one more day,' I replied

'That was a short vacation,' Tob said.

We knew that we both gasped at the thought of going back.

'Here we have a reason to celebrate then, you guys won't be with us for long, so let's party.'

'Sure lets go get drunk and dance to break some floor,' Bee said looking super excited and all of us walked up to the dance floor.

We danced till the last beat of the last track, it was 3.00 am already. We decided to go and sit on the beach for a while. Matt and Will also joined us to the beach. Matt played a few oldies in his guitar while rest of us hummed along his melodious tunes. After a long jamming session we wanted to return to our shack.

'How would you guys get back?' Tob asked

'We hired a bike'.

"You must be kidding me Nora". After 6 pints, you would want to ride a bike carrying a pillion, that to a drunk one. Are you serious?' Tob asked sarcastically.

'Come with us, we are anyway going back to Arambol, got to meet a few friends, I would ask Matt to get your bike' Troy said.

'Thank you so much, said Bee.

I knew that she was not interested for a bike adventure. We walked towards the parking area. There wasn't really a parking lot but just the backyard of the local flea market where people used to park their vehicles.

Being so tired and taking an early morning walk to the parking altogether didn't go so well, it was exhausting but at the same time it felt fresh. I loved breathing the early morning air.

We reached the parking when Troy pointed towards a van saying "And there is my van, my baby, my only love". It was dark so the van was not clearly visible. As we came closer…

'Holy shit, what the hell is this,' that was an 8 seater mini truck, looked like a van. Actually I, rather we expected a single colored van, not this painted 8 seater vehicle. There were sketches and designs scribbled all over the vehicle. One side of the van said "Decibels" written within a peace symbol sketch. The whole thing looked colorfully weird.

We all hopped in. Tob took the front seat with Troy, the Driver, Bee and I the middle seat and the other two occupied the last one.

Chapter 10

It was noon; I opened my eyes and heard Bee singing out loudly from the bathroom.' Bee come on, what did I do to you? May I know the reason for this musical torture?' to you? May I know the reason for this musical torture?'

'Nora, it's a new day, can you feel the love in the air?' Bee shouted.

'Love in the air? What the hell. No I don't feel anything in the air, now can you please stop shouting your lungs out,' I replied struggling to get my sleep back.

"Nora, don't be a jerk, get your ass out of the Bed. Everyone is waiting for us, check your bloody phone", she thundered this time.

'Who everybody?' I wondered and searched my phone. One of the texts from the lot said "Meet me, waiting @ Buddha palace". It was from Tob. 'Here it is,' so I exchanged numbers when I was drunk last night.

Yes, you shared mine too and he gave me a call some time back,' your guy is already there and quite possibly hitting at another chick. So can you please get up, at least for the sake of that?'

'Yes definitely, wake me up once you are done with your shower,' I replied and tried to sneak for a nap.

We went to Buddha Palace, everyone was already seated and they were having their lunch when we reached. We walked up to the table, wished them and joined them for lunch.

Troy came out with an idea. He suggested as they had no engagement for the next twenty days in Goa they should go to Bangalore to meet their friends and visit nearby places and try to find a suitable spot for organizing an event. They would visit Gokarna on their way to Bangalore.

'And Nora, Bee, we would like you guys to join us. It's going to be fun'.

'But we already have our tickets done,' I said.

'How does it matter Nora, we can always cancel a ticket. We get to spend some time together, we can see a place on the other hand, and we will reach Bangalore tomorrow before your flight lands, 'Tob said trying to convince us.

'And Troy, is it your colorful chariot that will take us back to Bangalore,' I asked.

'Yes Nora, you are correct,' he replied.

'No ways!!!! I am not going.'

After an hour we loaded our luggage in the van and started the journey towards Karnataka.

We had a plan of stopping by Gokarna. It is a beautiful place full of temples and the beach is really wonderful and it comes on our way back. We would visit the beach, relax there for a while and then drive back to Bangalore.

'Till what time do we reach Gokarna?' I asked. 'It would take us nearly four hours. We are planning to watch the sunset at the beach.'

'It's getting boring, dude play something,' Tob said to Matt.

'Yupp. What do you want me to play? Any request?'

'Anything,' said Tob.

'Hmmm. Ok, hotel California would do?'

'Yes hotel California it is,' Bee and I shouted in sync.

Matt started playing … On a dark desert highway.. Cool wind in my air…

We all started humming with the tune and finally ended up jamming. It was hot outside and the A.C in the legendary van wasn't working. We were literally exhausted. It was 4.30 in the afternoon and we were still driving through South Goa.

"Dude where did you get this thing from, the van"? I asked Troy with frustration

'Well I bought it the year I arrived in Goa.'

'So you are not from Goa?' I asked

'No. I am from Ludhiana.'

'Are you a Punjabi?' I was shocked.

'Yes, I am a Jatt.'

'I don't believe this. Ok, now I get it, so this is all about your dreadlocks, isn't it?'

'Matt and Will, what about you?'

'We are from Goa,' they replied.

'That's great.' I said and turned towards Tob and found him taking a nap. He was sitting beside Troy who was driving and it was risky because sleep is infectious. It was very much possible for Troy to feel sleepy if he noticed Tob sleeping. I thought of waking him up, and then I realized, 'wait…let me take few pictures before I wake him up,' he looked damn innocent and I somehow felt like capturing him. I switched my camera on to click him but after a while I was forced to take Matt and Bees clicks, with all super heroic poses. Wonderful!! This couldn't be more horrible a pastime.

The van was moving with a speed of 40 kms per hour. Honestly it didn't look as if it was in a condition to move faster. But Troy was giving his best with it you know.

'See this, we reach Canacona, not much of a distance left to cross Goa and we enter Karnataka,' said Troy feeling relieved.

Within seconds of Troy expressing the feeling about his upcoming victory of driving this useless block of good for nothing van, we felt few jerks and it violently came to a halt. He tried to start it for a few times, but no luck.

We all were staring towards Troy with amusement.

'What, don't look at me?' I guess that's the engine, it's heated up.

'Have we got some water there Matt?' Tob asked

'Yes, we have two bottles which we can.'

We all jumped out of the van to have a glimpse of the place till Tob and Troy cools their super-hot piece of shit.

We waited and waited for the van to cool down. After getting tanned for an hour or so, we resumed our journey towards Gokarna though we knew we would miss the sunset.

We didn't have much time left for the sunset and Troy pressed the accelerator to increase the speed. We just hoped to reach our destination safely without any more uncalled for incidents.

I started feeling sleepy and I closed my eyes. A while later I felt someone holding my little finger. Definitely it had to be Tob as he was the one who was sitting beside me. Wait!! I must be dreaming. He won't be holding my little finger. Why would he?

I got up to check if it was for real, oh Man, it was for real. My little finger was entangled with his and then I realized I was resting on his shoulder. I struggled to straighten myself on my seat. I pulled backed my finger but Tob didn't let it go. I looked at him but he smiled at me and said," Nora, I don't know why, but it feels so nice, holding you close' and he tried to hold my hand. I put my fingers within his and tightened the grip; he took a deep breath and thanked me.

'You need not thank me. Let me confess, I like you, I feel good when you are around and I keep looking for you, when you are not. I don't know, it was a short span spent with you but it feels like I have known you for days and I think you are the one for whom I have been waiting.'

He leaned forward for a kiss on my lips, but he held himself back and placed one on my forehead. We were so much into each other for a while that we never realized when we crossed Goa and entered Karnataka.

"It's already dark and we were completely exhausted. Let's stay at Gokarna for the night, we can see the sunrise tomorrow morning and continue," Troy said.

'Completely makes sense, provided it is safe,' I said supporting Troy. Actually we were so tired that we looked like zombies; staying back for a night looked like the only sensible option we had.

It was 8p.m. by then. It looked like a no moon day as I didn't see any clouds covering anything. We played few songs at a low volume and enjoyed the drive. We drove in the highway, crossing few towns and villages. It was late so, most of the shops on the way were closed.

The road was narrow and covered with cliffs and hills on both the side. Just lying back, being beside Tob and enjoying the night drive made me feel a bit relaxed. And the good part was we would have a place to rest tonight rather than dozing in the van.

We drove through and we were about to reach the river Kali when the Van started jerking, few jerks here and there and then, the Van stopped. Troy made a few attempts to make the damn vehicle run but it was an exercise in futility. He tried it again, but without any success. He looked at us, his face was anxiety written all over it. But he was not the one to concede defeat.

"Let me check it," he said and got down to check what went wrong. 'What's wrong?' Tob shouted out.

'Nothing much Bro, just give me 5 minutes, I would fix it very quick!!' Troy replied.

We weren't able to sit inside for long time and we came out to join Troy. It was 9. 30 p.m. by then, he had already taken 45 minutes for a very quick fix.

'Dude "Troy", you know what; I don't think you can fix it, let's search for some help,' Bee cried in frustration.

"I think Bee is correct we should get some help, you guys, be here and let me and Matt go and if we can find a mechanic," Tob said.

That was the highway, at the middle of nowhere, so there was very little chance of getting any help. In spite of being in a desperate situation, I began to laugh looking at them, so did Bee and Will.

'Common guys, not my fault,' said Troy.

Meanwhile Tob and Matt retuned, 'Guys, there is a garage at the other side of the bridge. We won't get any help right now who would give us a hand; I think we will have to do some manual pushing work to take the van to the other end.'

We, the girls, sat inside and Matt took care of the steering and the other three started pushing the van to take it to the garage.

It was a long bridge and it looked as if it would never end. The water beneath looked black, and that is the reason it is named as river Kali. The road was not at all crowded, and we could see very few vehicles crossing us. There were no people around, and the place looked horrendous.

They kept pushing the van till we reached the other end of the river and all of us took a deep breath. Still we had half a kilo meter more to garage (as per the information given by a passer-by). We thought not to rest till we reach the garage.

After 30 minutes of hard physical effort and mental exhaustion we finally found the garage. It was a small one; it didn't have much stuff in there but just the basic things.

We saw a boy fixing a bike; he looked at us for a while and then got back to his work.

"Hey dude, this thing doesn't start up, can you help us here?" Tob asked.

"Let me check it first?" The boy replied in English and opened the bonnet to check it. We all looked at him with anxiety and hope.

"Ok, it seems it's the oil filter. Don't worry; I can fix it, will take an hour he said again with an accent. You can sit inside till I am done."

"Oh no we are fine here," Troy said.

It was already 10.30 p.m. "Hope we get a place to spend the night," I said feeling concerned about the night.

"Yes, you should get something at Karwar. It is 4 kms away," the boy replied.

"But we are heading to Gokarna. I am sure we would get a place there too?" I asked.

"Yes, but its quiet late. You guys can stay at Karwar and carry on the journey to Gokarna tomorrow, anyways your choice", he replied.

"Oh. How far is Karwar and what is your name by the way?"

"It is 4 kms from this place. You guys would have crossed Karwar to reach here, and I am Jay Kumar."

"Oh shit... Nice name Jay Kumar and you speak good English."

"Thank you. Didn't continue my schooling though, learnt it by myself."

"Is it so? Boy, you are a genius. Why did you quit your study?"

'My dad used to take care of this garage; few years back he died, then I had to work here and take care of my family.'

'I am sorry.'

He smiled. "I will have to change the filter; it's not in a condition to be used," he said and got back to work.

We waited there as he fixed the filter, meanwhile discussing and planning about the rest of our journey.

We decided to visit Gokarna the next day early in the morning, enjoy the sunrise and drive back.

"Hey guys, it's done, Jay Kumar shouted closing the bonnet, you can move now." He took the key and started the van and luckily the machine began to work.

We thanked him and moved back towards Karwar. After a few kilometers of journey we reached Karwar town.

There was nothing open, but we were able to spot some guest houses. We started looking for a hotel that would be safe and comfortable. We didn't see anything of that sort.

"Let's do one thing, let's go towards the outskirts, I think we might get a Resort to put up," Tob said pointing towards the way out of the town.

We drove for a few minutes and then arrived at a resort named Hill view. It looked like a nice one. We parked the van and walked up to the reception to know if rooms were available. They had wooden villas available and we booked three of them.

Two of the hotel crew helped us carrying our baggage to the rooms and we followed them. All the villas were aligned together. I and Bee, took the first one, and the rest two were occupied by the male members.

After the tiring journey everything there looked beautiful. The villa looked quite comfortable. The rooms were decorated with paintings and fluorescent lamps.

Ring Ring. It was Tob, I answered the call.

"Hey Nora, I wasn't sleepy and thinking of taking a walk, would you like to join me if you aren't sleepy yet?"

'Sure, I mean I would love to. Give me 10 minutes, I would be there.'

"Cool, I am waiting," he said.

'Bee, would you like to join me for a walk?' I asked

'That would be the last thing I would like to do now, Let, me sleep, lock the door from the other side and please my dear Nora, don't wake me up till morning,' she replied.

"Sure. See you then. Good night" and I walked out.

I saw Tob waiting in the garden that was just in front of my room.

"Hey Tob, aren't you sleepy?"

"No not yet. It was a tiring day, and that is not making me sleep. I tried sleeping but kept staring at the ceiling. Nothing worked, that is when I thought of spending some time with you might make me feel better. Hope you didn't mind me asking you for a walk at the mid of the night."

Oh no, not at all. Even I wasn't sleeping. In fact I should thank you for asking me to join you. We started taking a stroll around the garden.

"So, tell me about you, Nora?"

"About me? Ha-ha, what do you want to know Tob?"

"Nothing specific. Just usual stuffs."

"Hmm, hi, I am Nora. I am from Kolkata, put up in Bangalore. I work for an IT lab. I love music. Bee and Books are my best friends. Travelling is my passion; my dad says 'the more you travel, the more you realize your own self', I believe in that. Taking up challenges and facing it gracefully is what life is for me. I love trying new things because I feel life is too short to regret or to fear. Ok, enough that's it!! What about you Tob? Tell me about you?"

"Well, you know quite a lot about me, my place, my work and even few of my stupid friends".

"Yes, I know them, especially the mental head "Troy", can't forget any of them."

And we laughed.

'Jokes apart, they are really good people. Tell me how did you meet these guys?' I asked.

'Ah! That is another interesting story, would you like to listen about it.'

'Yes, I would love to.'

'Troy and I met somewhere around 2 years back; I visited Goa with a few of my friends for a trip. We stayed at Arambol for some days. One evening I was partying with my friends, when suddenly few guys who were sitting beside our table, started hitting someone. The one who was getting hit was Troy. There was another one trying to pull both of them back, that was Matt. I didn't know him then, but I just felt like I should stand up for him. I tried pulling that other guy back. And finally he was off Troy. He was badly hurt and bleeding, their room was a little away from where we were. Looking at the situation I asked both of them to stay in my room for that night and Matt agreed. I and Matt carried him to my room. We got him some first-aid and medicines and let him sleep while Matt and I joined in for a drink.

'So what happened, why that guy was thrashing him to death,' I asked.

'Well nothing much. Troy kissed that guys girlfriend,' Matt replied.

Jesus. I would have known that before getting him to my room, I replied.'

This is how we met and about working together, these guys were already into events and I joined them after a few days. That is our story,' he said and took a deep sigh.

'Goodness me, something like this was expected from Troy,' I said.

We continued walking and talking about odd things. Everything was so perfect, the sky looked very clear and the stars were twinkling like disco lights, there was no sign of rain.

'Let's go search constellation in the sky,' I said.

We sat together, looked up and started counting stars looking for constellations; we were able to find Orion, arrow and bow, rest of them was just assumptions.

"It's very late; I think we should go and rest for a while. And we also need to start early in the morning,' I said and got up to walk back to my room.

"Nora, wait!! Please don't go and he pulled me towards him holding me tight.

'It is not even a week we met, but still I think we know each other for ages. I like spending time with you, sharing things with you, and I feel happy when you are around.

Is it that I have started liking you or something else?' he asked.

Deep inside I liked it, Yesss!! I was definitely fascinated with whatever was happening and wanted Tob to speak more about his feeling, but having a cool head, I preferred not to react.

"Tob, I like spending time with you too, but I don't know. Isn't it too early?"

We kept looking at each other in silence for a while thinking what it might be. Well, both of us were not willing to accept the truth. Tob broke the silence.

'Forget it Nora, this cannot be love. After all it's just a week, which is not enough to assume that we are in love, right?'

"Yes, quite possible that we are not in Love", I said, but what I felt was completely different.

"I love you moron, don't you see that", and that was the 3rd time I was biting my tongue to choke those words from coming out.

Silence again. After a while, "I think you should go take some rest now," he said.

'Yes, I should leave. Bye, then, goodnight.'

'Goodnight and thanks for giving me company.'

I walked towards the villa. I was about to reach there when I heard someone walking behind. I turned around to check, and it was Tob. He rushed to me, took me his arms, held me tight, whispering by my ears

"Nora, please don't, please don't go. I love you. I do. I might not be great at expressing this to you, it might sound very filmy and raw to you, but believe me; I have never felt this way before. Please be mine. I will keep you happy; I would never let you go, never ever."

"I love you too Tob."

That was a beautiful night. There was some kind of magic in the moment and I loved the way it was turning out to be. It looked like a dream.

Chapter 11

Knock Knock!!

We heard someone knocking hard at the door.

'Goodness, Nora, Could you please attend this?' Bee said.

'Please, you know I slept late.'

"I never asked you to go for a romantic walk, now please get yourself off the bed," Bee shouted.

I got up and opened the door. There was Troy with a wide smile. "You guys ready?" He asked.

"Go away and let us sleep."

"Nora its 4.30. We want to watch the sunrise at the beach. Come on, get ready," he said.

"Okay, give us 15 minutes", and I shut the door before he said something else, but still his voice broke into my ears "I am waiting out here Nora".

We loaded our bags back into the van and started towards Gokarna.

It was 5.45 when we reached Om beach. The beach is "Om" shaped if you see it from the cliff. We were lucky enough to reach just before the sunrise. We all jumped off the van even before it came to a grinding halt and ran towards the beach. The sea is at a lower level and we had to climb down a cliff. I rushed to take a position to capture the dawn when rest of them took theirs, to enjoy the scene. It looked so amazing and peaceful that I was just able to hear the sloshing waves, but nothing else.

We sat there enjoying the enthralling view till the sunrise. Then we started our journey back to Bangalore.

It was 8.00 p.m. when we reached Bangalore. They dropped Bee and me near our apartments and proceeded to their friends place.

After reaching back, there was literally no energy left within myself to do anything else but just to crash on my bed. The next day was a working day and I had to take proper rest.

I was just about to sleep when my phone rang. "Hey it's Tob, you sleeping? Did I disturb you?"

"No, not at all. Tell me," I replied.

"Oh, nothing, it's just that I, I was missing you."

"I miss you too."

We went talking for hours over phone never realizing it was 4 o'clock in the morning. Well, that was new. I didn't like spending time over phone.

"Tob, we should take some rest, it's late."

"Nora, 5 minutes more? Please.'

Next day office was not that great. After an enthralling holiday, the working day seemed boring and long.

I was making myself a coffee when Angela came to me and asked, "Where were you both?" she was looking quiet dull that morning.

"Will tell you later. What happened, you look sick dear?"

'I am getting engaged.'

'What the hell?' I shouted. 'When did this happen?'

'This happened when you guys were getting yourself tanned, may be.'

'Well congrats, that's good news.'

'Oh really?' She said giving me a strange look.

'So when is it? How is the guy? Where is he from? Did you inform Bee about it?'

'Nora, take a breath. Will tell you everything, for now what you guys should know is that, the ceremony takes place on Thursday, you guys have to come.'

'Definitely we would.'

Well that was a real surprise. When Bee knew about it, she was excited too.

I came back to my cubicle when I heard my mobile ringing. But before I could respond, the phone got disconnected. There were missed calls from Tob and a text saying "call me when you see this."

I thought of calling him during lunch hour so I put my phone back and engaged myself in work. After a few minutes Tob called again.

'Hey, how are you?' I asked.

'Where are you, Nora? I have been trying to reach you for an hour.'

'I am at work, I was about to call you Tob.'

'Ok. Cool, at what time do you get over with your work?' He asked.

'I would be free by 6pm.'

'So, we meet by 8.00? I would send you a cab to pick you up by 7.30 and bring you here,' he said.

'Ahh, Is there anything special?'

'Nora, baby there is nothing special. It's just that I am missing you and I want to see you.'

'Aww. Sure. See you in the evening.'

The cab arrived sharp at time. I wasn't ready and made the cab wait for 20 minutes. I knew I was getting late but didn't want to compromise with my looks. So I very carefully selected my dress, did a touch up and worked a bit at looking good.

The traffic was as usual heavy, and it took some time to reach the place.

'Hey Nora, where have you been and where is your phone?' Tob asked as soon as soon as he saw me.

'Oh, it's in my bag. Why? Did, did you call me? I am sorry, I stammered.'

'God! Nora, you are so careless.'

I said,' I am sorry.'

'Forget it. Let's go.'

It was an outhouse, seemed like one of his friends property. It was beautifully decorated. The rooms were spacious and chandeliers were hanging in almost all the rooms. The lights were dimmed.

'Where is Troy, and the other two?'

'They have been to a friend's place; I stayed back because I wanted to spend some time with you.'

He took me through the hall, up the stairs to the terrace. The terrace was quite a big area, there was a swimming pool at the right, a mini bar in the corner, the pool was decorated with floating candles and flowers; there were two chairs and a table decorated with flowers, laces and linen, a number of delicacies, and the champagne completed the treat.

He switched on the music system with some Buddha bar lounge, lighted a candle and placed it on the table. He pulled a chair for me as a gentleman, poured some champagne for both of us and then took his seat. I was astonished with whatever was happening.

'So what's special?' I asked taking a sip of my drink.

'We both are together, isn't this special,' he replied.

I was excited and happy at the same time. After all I always dreamt about a relationship like this, it looked like a fairy tale but then I somehow didn't understand how to react to that situation.

Honestly, I felt like getting my shoes off and start dancing but no, I didn't want to show my feelings, but then it would look bad if I didn't react at all. It won't do justice to his efforts.

'Tob, thank you for making me feel very special.'

'You are my princess. Let's have dinner, it's late,' he said and served my plate while I kept looking at him. I just loved the way he was.

Just at that time I received a call from Bee. I was about to answer her call when Tob snatched my phone and switched it off, "let it go, hope its fine if you speak to her later?" he said.

'Yeah. I think there is nothing urgent; I can speak to her later.'

We had a lively conversation. Tob used to speak lot, provided he was in the mood to. He kept on speaking and I was just enjoying the way he expressed himself. Well, he was hypnotizing or whatever it was, I was spell bound.

After we had our dinner, he asked me for dance, and it was like a dream come true.

We danced for a while. Then he held my hand and led me towards the pool. He knelt down facing towards the pool and asked me to do the same. I followed him. He then pointed me to a few flowers floating in the pool and asked me to pick one. There were roses, red, yellow, pink and white ones. I stretched my hand to get the white one and he smiled at me saying "Nora you are so predictable."

I picked up the rose and I found a note attached to it that said "open my petals". I plucked few petals to open it and "OMG" there was a ring inside".

'Tob, are you trying to propose me?'

"Nora, I love you. Please be mine" he said and put the ring into my finger.

I was short of words. I held him in my arms and said,'I love you too Tob. Thank you so much.' As it was very late, I decided to spend the night there and return in the morning.

Chapter 12

'Get up princess.'

I woke up and saw Tob sitting beside me.

'Tea time. Look at this, I prepared some real yummy tea for you,' he said

'Oh, don't be so nice to me, it is not required.'

'Well I am not trying to impress you or something. I am just trying to work on my cooking skills,' he said and handed me a cup.

The tea tasted awesome. Not sure if the reason was the tea or the one serving it, but it did.

'Where is your cup?' I asked.

'No I don't like tea or coffee or anything of that sort.'

'Oh, and you did this just for me?'

'Don't you want to go to work today? 'He asked with his wonderful smile.

'Yes, I forgot that it is a working day and I have to go to office. I don't feel like working today. Let me just apply for an off. I want to spend the day with you.'

'Sure, now get up from the bed, go and get your shower till I make something for breakfast,' he said and moved out.

I walked straight up to the bathroom turned the shower on to avoid any noise, and stood still beneath it looking at the mirror.

A whole lot of things ran through my mind.

'Is it a dream, if it is for real then what's next? He really loves me, doesn't he?'

I kept on thinking for a long time standing still in water.

'Nora, it's been ages you are in there, are you fine?' he asked knocking at the door.

'Yea, I am done. Give me 5 minutes'

I hurriedly got ready and ran towards the dining hall. He was already seated and I joined him. There was bread the brown ones, sprouts, oats, juice, milk, beans, nuts and fruits. "Yuck" was what I felt looking at the breakfast table, but with Tob I knew I had to have my breakfast properly and that was a better option rather than answering to his impossible questions.

Fruit was the only thing that I liked, so I picked up some fruit salad before he could get me any other tasteless stuff.

'Don't you have work today?' I asked.

'No, we have to meet someone. Need to discuss this event thing, but I had asked these guys to go and meet them. I won't be joining them today.'

'Isn't that important?'

'Yes it is but not more than you. I am sure these guys will manage,' he replied.

'Tob, please, I would like you to go for the meeting.'

'Never mind. Trust me, it's not that important.'

'I don't want to hold you back.'

'Ok, Nora, I would go if you insist.'

After Tob left, I switched my mobile on and went through the list of missed calls and messages.

Those were from mom, Bee, dad and few other friends and colleagues. 'Why is it always that you have a lot many people calling when you don't want anyone to call, but they won't call you when you are really free to speak?' I wondered.

I called up mom, spoke to her.

I also thought of calling up Bee when I remembered it was Angela's engagement the next day and we still had to do some shopping. That might be the reason Bee called me yesterday. I thought I would give her a call by noon and I turned off my mobile again.

I was so much into Tob and his magic around that I didn't even want to think about anything else. I cleaned the room, did a hair do, and put my best dress I packed with me while coming yesterday, trimmed my nails and waited for Tob.

For the first time I was happy waiting for someone. I kept on smiling at nothing but everything. What a beautiful feeling, I told to myself. I don't like spending time at the kitchen, but that day I enjoyed cooking. He was back in the evening.

We spent the whole evening speaking, sharing stories, he played for me, we jammed for a while sitting beside the pool.

The next day, I had to get up early. Tob was sleeping so I left a note for him "you looked so innocent while sleeping that I didn't feel like waking you up. Off for work, will try to see you by evening, love Nora."

Once I was in office, I rushed to Bee's cubicle.

'Nora, where were you?' She exclaimed when she saw me.

'Shhhh, I was with Tob.'

'God Nora, that's the reason you blush, now listen. This is disastrous,' Bee said with her eyes wide open.

'What happened, Bee?' I felt something fishy.

She was about to spill something when Harry came shouting "Girls, let's go, Angela's engagement party might have already started. God bless her with a good boy and us with good food.'

We joined him and drove to the party. That was an engagement party but that looked like a wedding. It was decorated nicely. Angela wore a peach colored gown and looked beautiful.

'You look amazing,' Bee said looking at her. We all appreciated her dress as it perfectly matched her. Angela was a little nervous.

'Hey don't be scared. You know the guy, right?' I asked.

'Yes that is one good part that I know him and he is my choice.'

'Then there is nothing to worry about. Everything is going to be fine. You never fail when you start something without expectation,' I whispered in her ears. After few seconds the ring ceremony took place. Everyone was quite happy, but Bee looked disturbed.

'What is it Bee,' I asked

'I would speak to you about it Nora. It's not the right time.'

We enjoyed the lunch and got back to work.

I didn't get time to speak to Bee that day. It was already time to go home. I was preparing to leave office when Bee asked me to wait for a while. I waited for her to finish her work and soon we were on our way back home. Just then Tob rang me,' Honey, how are you? When will you be back?'

'Tob, I am fine. I can't come today; Bee is staying with me tonight, got to be at home.'

'Ok cool, see you tomorrow then,' he said and hung up.

We returned back home and planned to go out for dinner. Bee informed me over the dinner that she was getting married. I was taken aback and said,' you are kidding me, aren't you?'

'No I am not. I knew it the day we were back from Goa. I wanted to tell you once it was confirmed. They confirmed it, the day before yesterday. I called to say you that, and you didn't pick up the phone. It is an arranged one, I have never seen the guy, and the wedding is taking place sometime in the next month. The date would be fixed very soon. He stays at Delhi and I might have to move.'

'Goodness me, Bee you are getting married. Congrats'

'Kidding me Nora? You can't be happy about this. You know how scared I am,' she said.

So you are going to relocate, right?

'Eventually, I would have to.'

'What happened to the world, why the hell is everyone getting married?' I asked.

'I told my parents I don't want to get married now. They say I don't have any option; the irony is they want me to get married, in short get laid with someone I don't know, if I want to see them happy,' she said

Funny isn't it, I said not knowing what else to say to her..

'This situation is called "confusion", not "funny", she replied with a sigh

'I mean, and yes it's confusing. I can understand.

That was a shock. We both had our dinner and got back home and went to bed.

Chapter 13

The next few days were busy ones. It was all about work, meetings and planning.

We did not spend much of time chatting in the cafeteria.

Angela got busy with her "would be" relationships, I started spending more time with Tob, and Bee, planning for her marriage still wondering what and how the hell it happened.

After few days, Tob and his group went back to Goa for their event.

I preferred staying alone though I knew I should spend time with Bee before she leaves for her wedding. We might not get those days back, but I never understood why I was being so selfish to ignore her and got myself so much into Tob.

It was about a Thursday evening when I was back from office, didn't have much to do, called up dad, called up mom, checked my personal mails. When I was done with all the usual stuffs, I lay on the bed looking at the ceiling. I was avoiding thinking of Bee but she started poking into my mind. Millions of things came into. I thought about the Kodai trip, the Varkala hide out; the deadlines faced together, the night outs we spent drinking and dancing, the flowers from Bee on 'Friendship days' every year.

Those would be gone after few days. She would be married. The main thing was that my close friend was getting married and I should help her in every possible way.

My mind was occupied with several things when the doorbell rang. It was my cook aunty; she is like a friend to me.

'What happened? You don't look well Nora, you look distressed? Hope everything is fine,' she said.

I was not feeling well and I wanted to speak to someone at that moment to relieve my stress.

I thought of calling up dad, I knew he is one person who, wherever is or whatever he would be doing, would listen to my nonsense and surely make me feel better. I was about to call him when Bee rang me up.

'Is your wedding date fixed?' I asked.

'Yes, that's on 18th of Jan,' she replied.

'And today is 20th of Dec, we have 29 days and when do you leave?'

'leaving on the 12th of Jan.'

'We have nearly 23 days left for your shopping, choosing your wedding dress and what not. So pack your bags for a week, you got to drop into my place tomorrow,' I said.

'Cool,' Bee said, she knew she didn't have any option rather than agreeing to my suggestion.

Bee was home next day morning at 8.00am. She kept her baggage in the bedroom and started getting ready for work. Both of us went to the office planning to return a little early because we were up for a rock concert that evening. That was a local band, those guys played good and we both personally knew them.

'It's been a long time we have not attended a rock show,' Bee said.

'Yes it feels like it's been ages,' I nodded agreeing with Bee. 'Remember there was a time when every Thursday we went to attend them and dance for hours on their tracks. Good old times.'

'Yes and the after parties with those crazy metal heads. That was fun. Nora, let us go have our time back,' she said.

As always, we reached the gig late and missed a few tracks, though it wasn't a big deal, it was not a linking park concert anyway. We took our usual corner that was the area near the speakers. We were in the habit of being late for the gigs but still managed to sneak into the front corner.

Bee liked dancing at the beats while I enjoyed the loud bass.

We started tapping our feet on their tunes which very quickly turned into "break the floor" dance. Sahil, the drummer noticed us and smiled at us. I was very glad to know that they still remembered us. Though we used to follow them and we were good friends, it was a long time for at least for rock stars to remember.

They were a band of three people; Corel was the bass guitarist, Max the lead and Sahil at the drums. The fourth one playing keyboard kept changing as per requirement.

Bee and I were in a party mood that day plus it was a weekend so we decided to stay till the gig was over. Thanks to the Govt. the closing time was 11.30, or else think what would have happened to people like us. We would be seen walking out early in the morning.

The band stopped playing at 11.30pm and packed their stuffs. The crowd at that place was a decent one so they started leaving quietly and so did we.

But at that time Sahil came forward and greeted us. After polite exchanges he led us to Max and Corel. We were very happy to meet each other after a long time. Particularly Corel was delighted and soon we were in her arms.

She was that bubbly girl whom you would like to meet over and over again. We walked up to the nearest cafe, took coffee and then Sahil dropped us at my place in his car.

I was not fully awake when I heard Bee sobbing.

'Bee, are you ok?'

'No I am not,' she replied with a whistling voice.

'Come on. Though I don't know what it is, I am sure things are going to be fine,' I said and gave her a hug.

'Nora, I don't want to marry. I feel sick. I don't love the person I am going to be with for the rest of my life. Not to speak of love, I don't even know him; she said and started weeping again.

'Bee, please don't cry, take it easy and it will be fine,' I said trying to console her.

Finally she stopped sobbing and said "let's go shopping" let me invite Angela too. She would be interested to join.'

She called Angela and as expected she was happy to join us. There was bread and eggs so I prepared few toasts for breakfast. After having our breakfast we got into a cab we hired for the purpose and went to the Mantri Mall for shopping. Bee wanted to get some cosmetics, sandals, and a lehenga (wedding gown) if possible; and Angela might shop for her wedding though she had time. When it comes to shopping, God save the girls. We reached the mall at noon; so, we opted to have our lunch before shopping. Bee is a foodie and the meal is always lavish whenever she is around. We discussed about Angela's wedding over the lunch.

'So the dates are not finalized yet?' I asked

'Officially, No. They say it to be March but then they would only confirm it only after it was approved by their "in-house" pundit.

'Bullshit,' Bee remarked and asked, 'How is your guy doing?'

'He is doing well. What about yours?'

'Well, I don't know. I can just expect him to be fine; mum and dad know them and in India that's enough for a wedding.'

We had our food and we visited all kind of shops- shoe stores, ornaments, ethnic wear, and what not. The search for cosmetics was very tedious and time-consuming as we were very meticulous in choosing the items. We tried each item to see if it perfectly matched her. After all she had to look very nice and attractive on her wedding day. The shopping continued till evening. We dropped Angela and got back home. We were too tired to talk; so, we silently took our dinner and went to sleep. I tried to contact Tob, but there was no response.

At midnight I heard Bee crying again. I tried to persuade her to stop crying and sleep.

Chapter 14

That was a lazy Sunday and we got up quite late. I checked my phone, had few missed calls but none from Tob that was heart breaking. I tried calling him up again but his mobile was turned off. So that was it, I felt like taking a flight right away to Goa to check what the hell was the person up to.

I kept on trying his number but then I found Bee swinging her feet to the accompaniment of music. She was the same person who was sobbing hard a few hours ago.

'Nora, come let's do this,' and she shook her butt twice to both the sides alternatively.

'God, Bee please, I am up to something.'

'Come on Nora, do this now and then you can continue playing with your phone,' Bee said pulling me to do that legendary booty dance of hers and also taught me for 10 minutes to dance along with her on that "abra ka dabra" Arabic tune that was provided to her by Harry. We danced along shaking our butt and swinging legs up in the air. The music was flowing and I felt as if I was Marjeena from Alibaba and forty thieves dancing in front of them serving drink when...crashh...

'OH shit,' Bee was on the floor.' Are you ok? How did you fall down?' Luckily she looked ok, forehead looked fine, no bone damaged, but the nose was bleeding a bit.

She grinned at me and said, "I fell down when you were trying to serve drink to the 31st thief. Let me get up and I will eat you raw Nora".

'I am sorry. Wait. Let me get you some first- aid,' and I plastered her nose before she could utter anything else.

That was 5.00 in the evening; we both sat on my balcony chatting.

'We still had some shopping left- lehenga, jewelries and sandal etc.' She said.

'Cool and what about the hen's party?' I asked.

'Hmm, let me think. A short trip to Pondicherry next weekend would do?' Bee replied.

'What the..I mean are you serious? This sounds awesome.' My insatiable desire to visit places would someday land me into trouble,' I thought. We spent the evening planning for the hen's party-booking hotel, tickets for the journey and other things. Although Angela was thinking of going to 'lake view holiday resort on the New Year, she agreed to accompany us to Pondicherry.

The Next day: place-Office

Those days we spent less time at work and more time shopping around. But the deadlines won't wait for the sake of someone's wedding.

On that day we had the weekly meeting with our Technical Manager, Mr. Phil to whom we report so far as our progress in work is concerned.

He listens patiently to all our problems, be it professional or personal, and tries to find remedies. In fact, he makes us comfortable at work place. He lives thousands of kilometers away from us but makes himself available at the time of need. He is a nice person but he never compromises with work; and gets furious if any of the employees fails to deliver.

'Bangalore guys, we don't see any progress here,' Phil said with a heavy tone.

Silence for a minute. We had to shut our mouth up because no one had started with the pending work list.

'So is it that you have not updated the status sheet or you didn't start?' he asked.

'Yes Phil, we have started with it, we didn't update the status yet, but will do it after the meeting,' I said.

We thought of completing at least some work after the meeting and then update the status by night. I thought he won't get to know about the fact that we had not yet started, and usually he asks us to update the status after the meeting for whenever we forget to update the status sheet; so, this should be cool. He-he, very smart, I looked at Angela and Bee with a "yes I did it" reaction.

That's what we thought, but the reality was something else.

'Which are the ones, tell me and I would update it in the sheet right away,' Phil said.

Bingo!!I looked up at others with my tongue out and they gave me a "you were the smart ass; now resolve this shit" look. I was simply baffled I didn't know how to handle the situation because I had for the one time resorted to falsehood.

'Hmm, the 3rd one is in progress by me; the 2nd is in progress by Angela and the, Ahh!! the 5th one by Bee. I replied.

Silence!! After a while when Phil was still trying to figure out what I said, Bee put the phone on mute and both of them started laughing out loud.

'Ok guys do one thing, get this done by tomorrow evening and update the status sheet. I would check it tomorrow at this time. We have promised our customers for this week, we can't delay it,' said Phil.

'Sure Phil' we said in a chorus and ended the call.

As soon as the call ended, ha ha ha, 3rd one in progress by Angela 2nd one by, ha ha ha, Bee started laughing the hell out. And when I looked at Angela; she was on the floor almost breathless holding her stomach. Well!! That was embarrassing.

It was already late in the evening so we decided to go back home and work overnight to get the pending work done by the next day. Angela wanted to join us at my place for the rest of the day. We were late, so we had our dinner at office and got back home for the late working sessions. We put our workstation in my bedroom, Bee at the chair, Angela at the bed and I took the bean bag.

We worked continuously till 1.30 a.m. getting exhausted until we literally felt like pigs. We thought of breaking the silence and taking a break. 'Work just for one whole night in a year and you would feel like you are worth getting the employee of the year award?' I was badly in need of a cup of coffee. But I found the coffee container in the kitchen empty. Coffee! At about 2 a.m. that to in a residential area! Impossible. We rang Harry and after several attempts he picked up the call.

'Hello Harry,' we shouted in unison.

'What the hell. Are you girls on fire?' he said with his sleepy voice.

'What's up?' Bee asked.

'It's nearly 2.00 am and it's a weekday, I don't sleep walk nor am I an undercover agent,' in short I was sleeping before you woke me up.

'Awesome, get up and drive us to the airport, please, please, please.'

'Bee; you can't do this to me, and who the hell comes at this late hour?' he asked.

'Surprise surprise!! Please come', Bee said.

She was finally able to convince Harry for the drive to the airport. He arrived within 20 minutes and we silently joined him and managed to keep him cool till we reached the airport.

He actually thought we had come to pick someone. We walked to a coffee counter at the airport, ordered for food and coffee and waited without speaking much to each other.

'Let me go get the order,' Harry said and walked to the counter.

'Bee, he is going to kill us when he knows we are here for coffee,' I said.

'Hmm, ok. don't worry let me think about something. Yes, just nod to whatever I say; try to follow me and act accordingly, replied Bee coming up with an idea.

'So who's coming,' asked Harry.

'Oh. A friend.'

'A friend of yours, this late?'

'Hmm, he comes from Dubai, Bee replied.

'Ok. So if your guest is a "he" then why can't he travel by a taxi? He said with a grin.

'Well, he is special.'

Meanwhile we had our food and coffee and at that time a flight from Dubai landed and people started coming out.

Bee, kept an eye on the arrival, and yea, she acted as if she was looking for someone. She kept looking for a while, almost everyone came out, she turned around and started weeping saying "he ditched me". I and Angela walked up to her to console her and pointed at a few remaining travelers to see if he was among them.

"No, he is not the one, not even him" she said weeping.

Harry was in a shock. When he got back to his senses he walked up to us and said "why don't you call him up Bee?"

"Do you think I wouldn't have tried reaching him? Why the hell would he keep his mobile on when he was in flight?" Bee cried out.

"But where the hell was he in the flight?" asked Harry

"Harry, please don't argue", I said, "don't you see she is heartbroken. Come let's go. Get the car".

'Poor baby, stop crying, everything would be fine. Come let's go.' I and Angela walked with Bee up to the parking and Harry followed us being awestruck.

Chapter 15

We were able to complete the pending work by next day noon and mailed Phil that we were done and now he could cool down.

Phil was happy with the work. 'Thanks and good job,' he replied on the same mail.

After a sleepless night three of us looked horrible. Just a day left and we had to start for Pondicherry. We had to complete the packing, few things to be bought before we leave and also the hotel bookings were to be confirmed.

That evening while I and Bee were getting our bag packs ready, I got a call from Tob. His name on my mobile display made me angry. I received the call saying "Do I know you sir? It would be great if you can help me because I don't have your number saved; neither do I have any clue about who you are."

'Huny, I am sorry, I am so sorry. I was busy,' he said.

'Where were you Tob? I have been trying to reach out to you for days,'

I asked getting frustrated.

'I lost my phone at the event that day. I got a new phone but I was waiting to get my old number back. I am sorry,' replied Tob.

I thought of saying a number of things to him but I just kept silent.

'Ok. Here it is. I know I have been a jack ass those days for being so careless, but I promise I would make it up. I am coming to Bangalore next week.'

That made me smile and I ended up saying him "love you" rather than a "get lost" which I really planned to say.

'So how far is this Tob and Nora affair going? Are you guys planning to take this relationship somewhere or just playing around,' Bee asked.

'Hmm, we like each other. Definitely not playing around but yes we have not yet decided on anything.'

"Definitely not playing around, this applies to both of you or its just you?" she asked.

I was stumped. I didn't know how to react. She put me in such a dilemma that I could hardly respond to.

'How perfect is that. You have the freedom to choose people you want to be in your life. Look at me, I am going to "most probably" spend my whole life with a person I hardly know,' she said and her smile suddenly disappeared.

'Bee let us speak about it. You have been avoiding this. Tell me what the issue is. Did you to speak to mum about it?'

I wanted to know what was going on but as she didn't say anything on her own, I thought it wouldn't be great insisting on her to share.

'Yes I spoke to Mum. What she had to say was "your dad has accepted the proposal, won't look good now if I deny and moreover it's the right time to get you married".

'Why don't you tell them that you are not yet ready?'

'Because in our caste girls get married soon, Mom's cousin's daughters are getting married, Dads best friend's daughter got married. Uncle's brother in law's daughter got married recently. Mom says it doesn't look good if I stay unmarried for long.'

She uttered those words in such a way that it made me laugh.

'I am sorry, 'I said realizing how sensitive she was.

'You jerk! It sounds funny to you.' Bee said and threw a pillow towards me.

And that made me laugh more and more.

That night I didn't hear Bee crying, it was a relief to see her sleeping peacefully. Probably she compromised and tried to accept it.

The next day when we entered office we saw someone looking very familiar to us.

'Hi Nora, Hello Bee, How are you guys doing?,' asked Cliff.

'Holy shit, Mr.Cliff is back,'I said to myself.

(Mr.Cliff is a dynamic personality. He is our reporting lead for the team here. He is a hard taskmaster and very intelligent and he hates the new-gen people. He thinks people in present generation take short cuts for success; they don't like to work hard, they prefer enjoying their lives more than working and number of other invalid assumptions. Well, this attitude affected our relations and careers too. In short he hated us.)

He was out on a business trip and unluckily was back on that day. We had thought of taking leave the next day. We didn't know how he would react when he came to know about it.

'Hey, nice to see you. How have you been, how was your trip? When did you come back?' I asked him as if I had not noticed him coming.

Meanwhile Bee stood like a statue. She too never expected to see him back that day.

'I am good, and the tour was great, will share few experiences in the team meeting today, and I also got chocolates for all of you, come, collect it from my desk,' he said.

Jesus, a team meeting with Cliff? That one hour of torture and you would somewhat feel like being at the mid of a tooth extraction without using anesthetic substance.

'Sure we would come in a minute,' we replied and walked away.

The meeting was still going on beyond noon and we were very hungry.

He told about all random things, he spoke about the journey, about the food, the work culture and what not. Finally after one hour and fifteen minutes, the meeting came to an end and we all took a deep sigh.

We were about to leave the meeting room when he called us.

'Nora, Bee and Angela could you please stay back and join me for a while, need to speak to you guys.'

Fish!!! Three of us took our seats in a corner while rest of them walked out of the meeting room.

'Let's not beat around the bush and come directly to the point. I see in the team calendar, you guys are on an off tomorrow,' he asked.

'Yes. It's a common friend's wedding,' Bee replied and we both nodded.

'Did you apply for it in the portal?'

'No, we updated it in the calendar. Moreover you weren't there so we thought we would send it to you once you are back.' This time I said and the other two nodded.

'That can be considered as an excuse, Look, I don't have an issue if you guys have to take an off but it's not fair on your part if all the team members (all means only we three working a project) to be on leave together. I can't let all of you guys to do that.'

'But not always we take an off together, and it's a coincidence. We don't plan vacations together,' I replied.

'Whatever it is I don't care. I want you people to sync up with each other before you apply for a leave from the next time, make sure leaves don't overlap and for tomorrow I want any one of you to be available,' said Cliff.

'We are moving out of station tonight, and we are definitely not carrying our laptops with us. We won't even be able to connect to the office network,' Angela said.

'Well, that's your problem. I don't care about how you manage.'

That was it; there was no use requesting him, and so, we dispersed without saying anything else.

Thanks to bloody Cliff, we had to carry a laptop with us. We decided to carry one and use the same within us to cover the work from home.

The bus started late in the evening. That was a private one and they didn't look alike, this time it was much easier to find the bus, we didn't have to search for it. The bus started late. It was just a six hour journey. We sat silently feeling the "Cliffs heat" and after some time we slept.

Next day we reached Pondicherry at 7.00 am. We took an auto to the hotel which was a few kilometers away from the bus stop, at the center of the city and very near to the rock beach. The room we booked was on the 5th floor, nice and comfortable one; the best thing was the sea view, it looked awesome through the window. That looked tempting. We were not in a hurry to visit places in Pondicherry because it is a small place and three days were enough to see around, still we thought of planning something for the day. We decided to visit 'Auroville' first during day time and 'Rock Beach' in the evening.

We got ready within an hour and half, picked up a map from the reception and walked out to call for an Auto.

'Sir, Auroville?'

'Two hundred rupees mam,' the auto driver replied.

'What? It's not even that far.'

'Mam, it's the minimum charge.'

We were sure it was the fixed charge for the auto wallahs to loot travelers and they won't agree with anything less. So, we accepted the offer and started towards Auroville.

Both the sides of the road to ashram looked beautiful and green. That was the tourist season and so lots of travelers were seen on the road. We reached within minutes and started exploring the place. It was indeed a wonderful place.

It was a bit hot out there so we rested at the ashram for a while and entered a French restaurant to have our breakfast. In Pondicherry, one would see number of French restaurants, shops and hotels with French names like la creame, le senora and la what not.

'Mam would you like to place the order?' The waiter asked.

Yes, I would have some bread scrambled eggs, a bowl of fruits and coffee. I said.

Angela asked for an omelet, some toasts and pineapple juice.

'Hmm, please get me lasagna, a veg croissant, and a cheese omelet, one garlic toast with jalapeno dip and fries, and one watermelon juice,' Bee added.

The waiter stood speechless for a moment and then asked Bee,' is anyone else joining you mam, should I get a few chairs?'

'None of your business,' Bee replied with a grin.

Looking at her order it looked like three other people might join us. He noted the order, said sorry to Bee and walked away. We were talking when I suddenly remembered any one of us had to be working on that day.

'Shit, we were supposed to work today,' I said.

No one remembered. I was sure there would be few threatening mails from Cliff in our outlook.

'Oh Yeah,' Angela and Bee cried in chorus.' What do we do?'

'Listen, I would have my breakfast and go back to the hotel and give the cover until you both see this place and come back. Anyway I have been here before,' I said.

'Are you sure Nora? We would like you to stay.'

'You guys know how Cliff would react.'

'Not required Nora. We can anyway give him an excuse,' Angela suggested.

'You are correct but just a matter of a day, right. Let's not start out vacation with weird mails.'

I had my breakfast and I went back to the hotel while Bee and Angela stayed back and returned to the hotel after seeing the place.

It was a wonderful evening; we sat at the rock beach, and enjoyed the splendid view of the sunset. We stayed there very late in the evening gossiping and taking ice-cream.

'Why is it that everything has to come to an end some or the other day? See one more day ends,' Bee said.

'Yes because something new appears to replace the old one,' I replied.

'Hmm. That is filmy, said Bee

And the ice-cream is awesome.' I replied.

'So Nora, share us the experience of working from Pondicherry, Angela asked and Bee joined her "oh yeah. How can I miss that part, tell us.'

'Who the hell was working? I was sun bathing by the pool putting myself on online status' I replied.

'Holy, such a witch you are Nora,' said Bee.

'Well that Cliff deserves this,' Angela joined her.

'Sister, sister,' someone called up. We looked back and saw a few kids standing behind us. They were looking at me.

'What happened? What do you want?' I asked

They pointed me towards my hair and I realized they were looking at my green highlighted hair.

'Beauty, sister,' they remarked and laughed. Probably they thought it was something out of the world and an object of amusement.

'Yea, so what did you learn, hair is not always black. Go away kids. Go play. Get going,' I said politely. They went away. But my friends burst out laughing.

'Ha-ha, Beauty sister, Ha-ha,' said Bee clapping her hands and Angela at her usual position, lying on the rock holding her belly.

On our way back to the hotel we stepped into a French café for dinner. It was not very big, not even an elegant one. It looked like a canteen but a classy one and the menu was awesome.

I glanced at the menu for a while; the names appeared weird to me and I didn't know what to choose.

'Bee your department, I don't understand anything. Order for whatever you like to.' I handed the menu card to her. Bee looked at Angela who had already pushed the menu card and was busy with her phone.

She went through the menu very carefully looking at the list of pizzas and then ordered for something that we hardly knew or cared about.

Angela and myself weren't that big fans of pizzas. The Steward came back with a giant double XL sized pizza and placed it on the table. Would you like to have something else?

'No, that's more than enough,' we replied looking at the pizza with our eyes wide open.

'I ordered for a family size pizza, never knew it would be this big,' said Bee

'Didn't you ask the steward about the size?'

'No, I did not, I am sorry. I never thought this would come out to be this big.'

We started picking up pieces expecting to complete at least half of it.

We ate but it was too big to be consumed by three of us though it was yummy. As we felt very heavy and our walk back to the hotel seemed a long one.

Next day: I woke up at 9a.m. by the alarm. Hey Bee, I called but to my surprise I found Angela sleeping but Bee was nowhere around. I got up and looked out of the window, the roads looked busy and the weather nice. (It was a day before the New Year so looked like the city was in a celebration mood.)

'Good morning Nora. Where is Bee?' Angela asked waking up.

'Hey good morning. Hope you had a great sleep. I didn't see Bee around. She possibly might be hungry and might have gone for breakfast. And yes the breakfast ends by 10, so if you want to have your breakfast for which you have already paid a lot of your hard earned money rather than having vada and bhajji outside, then get ready.'

'Oh, give me 10 minutes I will get ready.'

We got ready and walked up to the restaurant for breakfast. We searched for Bee but she was not to be found there.

'Where the hell did she go?' asked Angela. She also dialed her. Her phone kept ringing but she didn't respond.

'Now this is weird. She is not receiving calls.'

'Let's finish up our breakfast, go back to our room, get ready and go out to find her.' Meanwhile Angela kept on calling her.

We hurriedly took some toasts and juice from the number of items kept for breakfast we expected to enjoy and rushed back to the room.

'Let me try from my number,' and I dialed Bee.

'Nora. No use of calling her. I found her mobile under the pillow.'

'What should we do now? Where should we search her for? Besides no one knows we are here.'

'Stop panicking Nora. Get ready. Don't worry she would be somewhere here. Will search her in the hotel first, if we don't find her here, we can see what to do.'

Yes, Angela was comparatively strong when it comes to face problems like this because she has a cool head.

Finally we were running around each and every floor of the 8th floored building searching for Bee. I looked at the pool, but she was not there.

Let's check the club, I said.

'Nora. You are in a shock. Don't put much pressure on your mind. Why would they open the club by the day?'

'Oh yeah. Let's go and ask the hotel staff. Some of them might have noticed us together while checking in yesterday. So, someone down there might be of help. We started speaking to people working in the morning shift. We met the guards as well. We came to know that the guard at the gate had seen her going out early in the morning with her purse and camera bag.

'God, if she had gone somewhere at her own then why isn't she back? It's late.'

'Let's wait for her. We can't do anything else,' suggested Angela.

We were already tired and so, we decided to rest at the reception for a while and wait for her. Possibly she was not able to find her way back.

'I am sure that won't be the reason, she is good at remembering roads,' said Angela

'Yes true, she has a sharp memory. What if she is kidnapped for ransom?' I said getting restless.

'Jesus Nora. Why would someone kidnap her for ransom, that to here where no one knows her?'

'Yes you have got a point.'

'That's common sense Nora, that's in you also too but unfortunately you are not using it right now.'

We were discussing on other possibilities when we heard that unique sound of anklets. We were sure she would be none other than Bee. We turned around and saw her walking towards the lift without noticing us.

'Hey, where were you?' I shouted and rushed towards Bee.

'What are you up to Nora? You look worried.'

'Yes because we have been looking for you for more than an hour.'

'OH. I woke up early; I wanted to go for a walk. You guys were sleeping so I thought not to wake you up and I sneaked out and went to the local market.

'Can't you carry you phone crazy woman,' Angela asked.

'I forgot to put it in my bag. I was almost in the market when I realized I had left my phone back in the room. I thought I would get back before you people wake up.'

'How can you rely on assumptions Bee? Anyways chuck it now. Let's go back to our room.' I said trying to cool it.

We didn't plan much for that day. We just preferred having lunch outside, roaming in the local market and spending the evening at a cafe near the rock beach.

Bee was feeling a bit restless and was not able to sleep that night. She sat by the window looking outside. Seeing her lost in her thought, I walked up and sat beside her and asked,

'What happened? Speak out; I am sure you would feel better.'

'It's nothing Nora.'

'Look. I have been noticing you since the day your marriage was settled and I don't think things are going that great with you.'

'OH! I don't feel good about, whatever is happening. I have no clue about what to do. They don't understand that

I need time. I am not yet prepared for the marriage. I am just, not ready for changes like this.'

'Hmm, Bee it might not be even that worse as you are suspecting it to be.

What if it turns out to be great? After all, they are your parents and they are concerned about your future. Whatever they are doing must be for your good.'

`   'What if it doesn't? I have already talked to mom. I can say 'no' without caring about her, but am just worried about the consequences. I don't want her to be upset about anything that relates to me. I am sure she understands me but it's about what others would think, it's about relatives and the foremost thing, it's about my dad. He wants me to settle with someone.'

'That's what fathers do. They think it to be their duty to get their daughters married at the right time. They want their daughters to be happy, don't they? Why don't you try and speak to your dad.'

'Look, I have never shared things with dad. I respect him for sure but I somehow never had that compatibility of sharing things with him, neither did he have the habit of suggesting me anything. We speak for hardly five minutes a day. It is mom who keeps things at place.'

'So speak to him now. If you have not done something till now, that doesn't mean you will never do it.'

She remained silent for some time and then said, "Forget it Nora. Will see what happens. Tell me what's going on with you and Tob? How's that crazy one doing? You people are in touch, right"

She asked trying to change the matter of discussion.

'Yeah, we are in touch. He's coming to Bangalore the week you leave for your wedding.'

'That's great. Just ask them to get a proper transportation booked and they better be careful of Troy.'

Both of us started laughing.

Chapter 16

That was the New Year's Eve.

We decided to visit a few places, go for shopping and attend the New Year party in the evening which was being held in the hotel where we were staying. But before that we had to go to the beauty salon for a hair do; so, we left after the breakfast.

We were in the salon. Angela went for a manicure and pedicure.

I requested for a base color to my hair.

'And mam what would you like to get done?' the girl attending me asked Bee when she saw her sitting by the chair beside and looking at herself in the mirror.

Bee didn't reply and she kept staring towards the mirror.

She wanted to get a haircut done and highlights. I replied her and turned to Bee. Probably she was not herself.

'Bee,' I shouted.

'Yes, Nora,' she looked at me as if she was shocked.

'Where were you? What happened? Are you fine?'

'Nothing,' she shook her head.

'Tell her what would do you like to do?'

She looked at her and said "I don't know and I don't care how I look. Do anything that would make me look normal.' She turned back at the mirror and said, "I look like a pig now."

There was a kind of indifference in her attitude towards everything which I had never seen. She had a positive attitude to life and very often she came to my rescue whenever I was in distress. But that day was different and I knew there was no use asking anything to her right then. So, I told the girl "it's a haircut and few highlights, you can start with that and we would let you know if we need something else."

'Sure mam,' she said and asked another girl to get the color brochure.

After a while Bee's phone rang and she received the call, saying "Hello. Yes I like it...sure, ok' and she ended the call.

I felt restless looking at her and asked the girl to leave us alone for few minutes. 'Tell me what is it now? Hope everything is fine..?'

'It was mom's call. They are out for shopping and she was asking me about ornaments. She sent me pictures, and wanted to know if I liked those. I told them I liked every piece of it without even looking at it.'

'Wow Bee...you are a lucky one, everyone's shopping for you. You should be happy.'

'Yes, I know I should be happy but somehow I am not, I don't feel like being happy about something I don't like. I am just lost.'

'Ok. Don't worry. Look today is the last day of the year. No one knows what's coming up next year. So, forget about all the worries and be happy for the present. Can you do that, at the least? Now let's decide on what colors do you want for your highlights. I picked the color brochure and went through the colors.

'I don't need anything,' she said getting irritated.

'Shut up and look at this.' At last she agreed and we left the salon there after.

That was an amazing evening. We took a walk through the nearby lanes where we saw almost everyone in the local market had decorated his or her shop or hub with different types of colored lights. The streets were crowded with shoppers and in the late evening of the New Year Eve, people were on their way to the hotels which looked grand with beautiful decoration to enjoy the celebration and welcome the New Year. We took a stroll around, came back and got ready for the party.

We didn't want to enter the club that early, but as we were already in a party mood and the club was just below the floor we stayed, we made it quite early to the club.

The DJ took up the console, people slowly came in, drinks started flowing in a routine manner and the night was gradually becoming a bit wild and ecstatic.

There were special starters, special bartenders, special drinks, special guests and what not and we as usual looked for a place very near to the sound system. The music was okay, it was a commercial party and the guest DJ was yet to come.

Angela and Bee looked for something to eat while I ordered some drinks for Bee and myself. The waiter got our drinks and asked us if we needed anything else.

'No nothing for now. Will let you know if we need anything else.'

Suddenly we were surprised to see Harry in the party.

'Oh! Harry. What the hell are you doing here?' I asked.

'Vacation with friends. Can I join you girls? It's really boring with those guys and this Bollywood music sucks.

'I think even you guys were bored too. Now you won't. You are lucky this evening to have Harry here to entertain you throughout the party. I didn't want you people to have a boring New Year eve. It would be fun to spend the time with you. He pulled a chair and sat beside me.

The place was getting crowded, all the tables and the counters were filled but the music was still not getting better.

And Bee shouted,' Lord. I don't understand what the DJ is up to. It's getting me flipped.'

Yeah dude. It's really pathetic" joined Harry.

'I guess it should be fine when the guest DJ takes over.'

'If this continues, I would rather go back to my room and watch TV,' said Angela

'Chuck it. Let's talk about New Year resolutions, trying to work on the boredom.'

'Resolutions, I haven't made one till now,' said Harry.

'Neither did I,' said Bee.

We all looked at Angela.

'I would do some savings and stop being a spendthrift, and what about you Nora.'

'That's a difficult one. And me, hmmm, yes, I would learn cooking so that I can cook at least my own food rather than depending on my cook aunty.'

'Aww...'Bee and Angela said in sync.

Harry thought for a moment and declared that he would like to write a book that year.

'What would you write on Harry?' I asked.

'Well, I would write real stories based on my experience of life but it would not be an autobiography.

'Ok, real inspirational stories from your life, you got to be kidding me Harry' Bee remarked and we all burst out laughing while Harry looked at us as if he would have thrown us out, had it been his club.

'What about you, Bee? Oh my God, you must be having a tough time to decide something. You are getting married and you will have to wait till your hubby decides or approves something for you, right?' Harry asked pulling her leg.

'Well, not exactly because I would not allow anyone, even if he were my husband, to curtail my freedom. This will be my resolution for this year,' said Bee.

The awaited guest DJ took over the console exactly at 10.30p.m., with high expectation we finished our drinks and walked up to the dance floor. But that didn't make much of a difference as he too continued playing some commercial Hindi tracks which was not our cup of tea. We tried hard to tap our feet up with the music for a while, but not for long.

'I think I won't be able to take it anymore. Should we be leaving?' I asked.

Angela and Bee agreed.

'It's going to be New Year after a while. You can't leave,' said Harry.

'This noise is unbearable Harry,' I replied.

'Cool. Don't worry. Let's do something else; you guys want to go to some other place, or coffee? Or may be for a drive?' he asked.

To be honest any of the options would have been better than where we were then. So, we were ready for the drive. Then we walked out of the rocking Bollywood party that was literally getting into our nerves.

'So, how are we going? We believe you got your car Harry?' I asked

'No I got my friends jeep. Don't worry it is a modified one with a short chassis. You guys gona love it for sure.'

He asked the valet to get the jeep while we waited for it outside the hotel.

After a few minutes, he got the jeep and we jumped in. Bee took the seat beside Harry, Angela and I occupied the rear seats. That was a windy and cold night; we covered out faces with scarf, drove through the city with the music system on in full volume. We also bought some fire crackers on the way from a shop that was still open. It was 11.30 and we could still see people on the roads. I thought everyone would be partying that night.

There are people who spend the New Year in different ways such as watching movies, going for group outing, spending time with children and enjoying good food etc. I had been thinking for some time to celebrate the day in an unconventional way. Why not with the deprived section of the society?

'Guys, let's do this, for New Year. Go shopping tomorrow morning, buy gifts and distribute them among the needy, or else we can also go to an orphanage to meet the children, present them gifts and try to bring cheers to their life though for a moment only,' I suggested. All of them agreed to my suggestion.

Meanwhile we drove out of the city towards Auroville searching for an empty lawn or a field to burst crackers at the countdown to the New Year but unfortunately we didn't find one. It was already 11.50; so we got down by roadside and unloaded the cracker bags. We placed fifteen flower crackers side by side in the open space beside the road and lighted them just at 12.

'Happy New Year,' we shouted and hugged each other. Meanwhile the crackers exploded scattering different colors in the sky. Some people living nearby who were out in the street also joined us in the celebration. We kept looking at the sky till the colors faded away.

The next day, harry picked us up at 10.00a.m. and we drove to the nearest mall. Harry had already collected few information about one of the orphanages, the number of kids, there age group and other details. There were twenty five children in the age group of four to fifteen - 11 girls and 14 boys. We had to get gifts for all of them. We bought new dresses, school bags, pencil boxes and drawing kits and chocolates. We got them wrapped, loaded them in the jeep and drove towards the place. The expenditure incurred was shared by all of us.

Harry had already spoken to them regarding our visit so we didn't have any problem getting in there and meeting the kids.

We walked up to the office led by an attendant. The director for the orphanage was a very sweet spoken lady. She made us sit in the lawn and asked the attendant to call all the kids. All of them came running and gathered around us; we distributed the gifts among the children. All of them in unison thanked us. That was such a pleasure to watch them smile while opening the boxes. Harry played with a few kids, Angela and Bee helped some of them in unpacking the gifts while I tried to capture all those moments.

Such an amazing new year it was. It was not merely an act of charity. In fact I loved those children. Whenever I met a street urchin, I would smile and talk to him or her and take a photograph. But for my profession I would like to spend more time with them.

We were done with the day. Harry dropped us back in the hotel. We just had that day to spend in Pondicherry and the next day we would be back to our same old life, that same old Daniel Drake, same old pathetic Mr.Cliff and same shitty meetings.

'Why do good things come to an end so soon?' lamented Bee.

We had nothing to do in particular. As Angela wanted to go for swimming, we accompanied her to the pool. Bee was scared of getting into the water and I didn't know how to swim. Both of us sat by the pool side while Angela plunged into the water and started swimming. I drank some lemon juice and read a few pages from a book by Shantaram. Bee was lost in her own world. We spent some time relaxing and then returned to our rooms.

'Bee, are you gona miss these things after your marriage,' Angela asked

Bee smiled and didn't respond to that but probably her response was not required. We knew what it was.

We stayed inside the hotel room till sunset and then in the evening we went out to take a stroll. The market looked crowded even that day; definitely, it was the 1st day of the year. The shopping part for us was already done, after meeting those kids I somehow didn't feel like getting something for me. While walking I noticed a small studio that was named as "memories" and suddenly something popped into my mind.

'Let's go get a photo of ours here,' I said.

'You got to be kidding Nora; I think you got a better camera than this guy has,' replied Bee.

'Believe me, this would be fun.'

I was somehow able to convince them for the pic. We walked into the studio when we noticed no one inside it. We called up for someone and finally a lady came out.

'We wanted to get a group photo clicked,' I asked

She handed us a brochure displaying the sizes and the sample of few pictures. The product specification part was fine in the brochure but the sample image attached to it was somewhat strange. It was the photograph of one tall, dark, odd shaped bearded person who was standing in front of a waterfall back-drop, with one of his hand in the trouser pocket and the other caressing his "simply beautiful" beard.

'Are those pics clicked here?' Bee asked after staring at the person in the brochure for a while.

'Yes mam, this was our first photo-shoot with a south Indian model,' the lady in the other side of the counter replied.

'And he is a model from south?'

'Yes mam, he is a very popular model.'

'Ok...' Bee said looking at us, 'guys I don't think it's a good idea.'

'Common, who cares how the pic comes out to be? It is just for fun. Let us give some real nice retro poses like our moms used to click shots,' I said

We asked for an A6 sized shot. She asked us to walk inside the studio. The room was a small one that had the waterfall background and the photographer had the most basic DSLR for his so called professional shoots. We wanted to have our photograph in a sitting position, so I asked him for a bench. They didn't have a bench but they got us 3 tools to sit on. We placed it together side by side and sat on them placing our hand on each other's shoulders, keeping a placid look at the face without any smile, to get it retro, and the guy clicked few pictures till he got his best shot. We just hoped he would do justice to the photo. The photographer requested us to wait for some time. We waited for him at the counter and after a while he came with the photo and handed it over to us. Luckily the photo came out to be as expected. We asked him to get a black and white copy so that it would have vintage look. We paid him for his work and walked back to the hotel.

That night was just about spending time with each other, chit chatting about various things.

'So the hen's party finally comes to an end,' Angela said.

'Yea, and also the end of Bee's singlehood,' I said.

'And this might be the end of my freedom too,' Bee joined us.

'That isn't; getting married doesn't necessarily mean you lose your freedom,' I said

'Yes. True. But getting married when you are mentally not ready for it would definitely take away my independence,' replied Bee

'Bee you are simply exaggerating things. Chill, things are gona be great,' Angela interfered.

'Yes guys. I am getting a bit hyper. The grass is always greener at the other side, isn't it?'

'Look Bee, even I am in the same boat. I too would be getting married somewhere mid of this year, even I don't know the guy personally, but I haven't that negative attitude about married life as you have,' replied Angela

'Yes because you are mentally prepared for it. You wanted to get married and settle down and you are doing it. But that's not what I wanted.'

'Cool. Then why don't you just say "No", Angela replied back in no time

'Because I can't. I don't want my mom and dad to be upset for me or hate me for my selfish reasons.'

'Accept the fact that you are scared to face the consequences,' said Angela

"There was silence for a while and then I asked "You guys done? Need some more time for Q & A?"

'We are done on this topic,' Bee replied and Angela nodded in agreement

'Morons..'

'Okay forget it. You tell me how is your new relationship going? All well. You like him?' Bee asked Angela.

'Yes, he is cute. He plays guitar, he sings, he is a family person and he seems to be good. Enough I think, let's see, you never know,' Angela replied.

'Awesome! So we get to know a rock star then,' said Bee.

And Nora, What are your plans? Angela asked turning towards me.

'No, not me now. You two please continue meanwhile I would get back to Shantaram.'

'She is another crazy lady. We are just confused but she is not even aware of what's happening.' Bee said and both of them laughed...Yes, they laughed at me.

So that was it. Next day, we boarded the bus on time and got back to Bangalore.

Chapter 17

It was a week after our return from Pondicherry Bee was supposed to leave and Tob was to come. He was gona be here for a week, he wanted to spend most of his time with me but then I had to plan for Bees wedding too. Lord, too much to do. I was in the habit of procrastinating; I kept my work (except office work) pending till the last moment which was reason of most of my undoing. I had certain arrangements to make for Bees wedding. She didn't know about it; she knew I was speaking about booking the tickets but she never assumed I had not done it yet.

We had mixed feeling during those days. Some changes were awaited, a few new relationships ahead but what mattered was that our enduring friendship would help us see through all the changes. And as someone close once said "Changes are for good, look at it that way and it will turn out to be the same".

Bee preferred staying at my place till her departure for her wedding. That was her hideout and I thought she didn't want to spend her time alone just to keep away her anxiety. As per her she was still not over with her hen's party and was having it on instalment at my place. Well, nice excuse.

Time passed faster than our expectation and there was only a day left for Bee to leave. Though she was going off just for a month but there was a feeling that she would be gone forever. Definitely things are not gona be same when she will be back and we might not have the same space which we used to share.

We thought of booking an airport cab to drop her but Harry took over the task.

'Common guys!! You can wake me up at midnight just for a cup of coffee but can't ask me to drop you at the airport for genuine reasons,' he said when he noticed us booking a cab.

'Wish you good luck. Don't think much. Be a good girl. Come back soon. Will miss you,' Angela said to Bee before leaving office that day. Her colleagues also wished her which made her feel more nostalgic and emotional. She asked me to go back home because she wanted to stay alone for some time.

'Back home,' Bee stop being so creepy.

'What did I do?' Bee replied.

'You are behaving weird. Look at yourself. What the hell do you want from your life?' I asked.

'I need nothing. That's the problem. I need nothing in my life right now. Not even from my new upcoming relationship that is coming from "nowhere". I don't need it right now,' Bee said with a frustrated tone.

'Look. The choice is always yours. You can have your parents wish come true or your own; you can just have one or the other and you can't have both, in short you have radio buttons.'

"I guess things would have been different if we had 'check boxes'."

"Jesus, okay listen to me Bee, do you want me to speak to Mimi?" I asked her being restless.

'No. I don't. Just, just leave it as it is. I think I deserve this. You just make sure you are coming to the wedding.'

'Oh shit, the tickets,' I murmured.

'Sorry?' Bee looked at me in bewilderment.

'No nothing. I have to get printouts for my tickets.'

'And Tob is coming to Bangalore, right? When does he reach? Why don't you ask him to accompany you to my wedding, I am sure he would like to attend an Indian traditional wedding. Invite him on my behalf.'

'He reaches this Sunday and I would surely ask him and will drag him too if he doesn't have anything else to do.'

'Wow, you guys are gona to dating and enjoying alone. What about me?

So you wanted to join us in our date or something? I said looking at her surprisingly.

Holy... I meant you guys would be enjoying while I would be under the marriage trauma. Forget it; let me check if I have packed everything.' She began to check her bags.

I thought of cleaning the room, but when I looked around, I literally didn't understand where to start it from. It was a mess. I thought it's better to clean it the next day after Bee left.

"Nora, this is for you," and she handed me a card.

I opened it. It was beautiful with almost all the colors in it, that said "thanks for everything" written at the top of the card. And inside it I saw 'will miss all the crazy little things we did, with love-Bee.'

'Well that was touching.' I hugged her and we started crying.

Next day morning was her flight. Harry arrived ahead of time to pick us up. Thanks to this guy for being available anytime. We put the bags in his car and drove towards the airport. Harry had this fascination of listening to old songs while driving and we were rarely allowed to change those. It started with "aapki naazaron ne samjha" that day.

'Holy shit, Harry could you please pass me the cable, this is making me sick,' Bee shouted.

'Bee!! This is classic,' replied Harry

'I know this is a beautiful track but I need something else now.' She was getting restless. She snatched the cable and connected it to her mobile phone.

We reached airport in time. Bee wanted to spend a few minutes with us before checking in. We took coffee and spent some time outside the departures. I tried to make her feel better,' don't worry baby, I would be there soon. Keep updating me. Text me and be in touch.'

'And you please reply to my messages.' she said sternly.

She hugged me and Harry and walked in. We got back to our car and drove back home.

Back at home: I again looked at the card and began thinking.' Is it all happening for good? What if things don't go well for Bee with her new relationship? What if it doesn't work?'

'No, things won't be that worse. Bee would manage. I think I am just being a little hyper.'

I decided to concentrate on something else, may be on Tob because thinking of Bee was making me nostalgic at times. I called up Tob to ask when would he be here and if he needed anything.

'No honey. It's just you. My flight reaches Sunday morning. Those guys had booked a resort for me, looks like a beautiful and eco friendly one, I am sure you would love it. I would pick you up from your place,' he replied.

'Are you coming alone? What about others?

'They are not coming. They got some other work. Mine is a college event. I would be accompanied by their in-house event group plus some local friends. So we don't require many people there to manage. I hope you are coming along with me, right.

'Sure. See you on Sunday.'

I packed my bag. I knew it was going to be a few days with Tob. I started cleaning my room just to try and concentrate on something else rather than Bee. I wasn't feeling that great. I chatted with Bee post dinner. Was just curious to know how things were with her.

Nora: Hey. How's everything there?

Bee: Pathetic, suffocating. Relatives at home. Haven't seen so many faces together till date.

Nora: Lol. Is everyone happy?

Bee: Why won't they be? They are getting free gifts as a part of the pre marriage ritual.

Nora: Common kid. Don't be so mean. It's good to make others happy.

Bee: Yes it is. Even at your own cost, isn't it?

Nora: How is Mimi, papa?

Bee: They look good and happy. Didn't have a chance to speak to them personally?

Nora: Convey my best wishes. And Tob is reaching tomorrow

Bee: Yayaya... fun time starts. Miss me.

Nora: He he. Sure. Go to bed. It's late. You need to sleep properly to look good on the wedding day. Goodnight.

Bee: Si...goodnight micara. Keep me texted.

Chapter 18

That night I finally booked my tickets for Bee's wedding. Next morning when I was still asleep my door bell woke me up. 'Please no. I can't get up.' I hardly slept last night I thought. But it still kept ringing. I finally woke up to attend whosoever he was. I suspected it to be my cook aunty. I opened the door rubbing my eyes. Oh my, Tob was at the door.

He hugged me before I could think of anything.

'Hey Nora, I missed you so much.'

'I missed you too.'

'Go get your bags. The cab is waiting for us.'

'Give me 10 minutes, I haven't even brushed my teeth yet,' I said and walked in to get ready.

The resort was some 40 kms away from my place. Tob was hungry so we stopped at a restaurant on our way to have our breakfast. Though not an Indian, Tob was fond of Indian delicacies. So he ordered for a Neer dosa and khara bhat.

'This college event is going to be a big one. I have to arrange an international DJ and a local band or an artist for these guys, and sound, and machine, and the setup, the décor, oh lord, help me I got to work hard. I hope you are helping me to get this done, right Nora?' he asked.

'Hmmm, I would love to help you Tob but I have to leave for Bees wedding and I also think it would be great if you can join me. She wants you to come along.'

'Sure. When is her wedding? I hope it's not next weekend.'

'It is next weekend; it's on Saturday.'

'Shit, that collides with the event, I am sorry love,' he replied.

'Oh, that's ok Tob. I had already told her about your busy schedule. So don't worry, she is aware of everything. I am sure she won't mind.'

We finished our breakfast and started going towards the resort. I was still not done with my sleep. I slept in the vehicle. The resort was located near a village but the area surrounding it was breath taking. The guys led us to our room. They had a beautiful executive room booked for Tob. I threw my hand bag in the sofa and jumped on the bed.

We went for a walk around the resort before lunch. I didn't know the reason but I was damn excited to be with him. There was something in him which attracted me towards him. I thought he was highly professional and my presence would not affect his work. Anyway he had nothing to do on that day. We spent the whole day lazing around not doing much but just being lost in each other. We had delayed uneven meals, late shower, skipped phone calls and messages; in short we were busy doing nothing important.

We kept our mobiles on flight mode; I don't understand why people do that. They can just say that they don't feel like speaking, there is nothing wrong in not being in a mood to speak. Well we did the same.

It was late in the evening when I thought of checking my messages. I was sure of a few from Bee and yes it was there.

Bee: Good morning. Day goes not so great and the sun is freaking out here.

Bee: It's my wedding but looks like no one is interested in me. Everyone's busy.

-Bee: ??Are you busy too?

-Bee: Cool. Reply back when you see this..

-Bee: you there?

-Bee: where the hell are you?

That was her last message. I thought it would be better to chat with her:

- Am with Tob. Phone was switched off. Sorry for the delayed reply. Hope everything goes well.

-Bee: Jack ass. I have been trying to reach you since morning. Where have you been?

- Out here at a resort. Tob wanted to spend some time with me and he picked me up early in the morning. He wanted me to switch my mobile off.

- Bee: Fucker. Well forget him. I had some time to speak to dad today. He just wants me to be happy and I am still confused, that's what he thinks of me, wait… or I am just not able to convince him that I am doing fine and happy?

- Why don't you tell him then that you don't want to move ahead?

- Bee: Dude. It's not even a week to go. I can't do this.

- Chill. Enjoy your wedding then.

- Bee: Stop tripping on me girl. How is your guy doing?

- He is doing well. I asked him if he could come over. But he is busy. And he also said he would have loved to be there.

- Bee: diplomat

- He isn't. He is just very French.

- Bee: Cool. You go, have your time with your French toast. I would go check out what's new.

- Ha ha. Cool. Catch you later.

I looked up closing my WhatsApp and I saw Tob staring at me.

'Tob, what is it?' I asked

'Nothing much, I was looking at the speed you type the text in your phone, is like 200 bpm.'

'Ha ha. And that wasn't at all funny Tob.'

Tob wanted me to stay there and spend some time with him but I would not be able to take leave from office because some important work was there to be completed by the week.

'I will leave by 9 am. Will see you somewhere in the mid of this week if possible.'

'What. You won't come back?'

'Honey, this place is too far. And I have meetings in the evening. Can't afford travelling so far, please try and understand me.'

'You want me to shift somewhere nearby? We can stay at my friends outhouse too if you want to?'

'Oh no. The college is near to this place, would be easier for you to work. And anyway I would try to see you sometime this week.'

'Ok, if you say so. He replied. But be in touch and remember I would be missing you.'

'It was 8o'clock in the morning when I felt Tob lying beside and caressing me slowly. Tob placed a kiss on my forehead as soon as I opened my eyes saying "good morning love. "How did you sleep?'

That was a wonderful morning. I wished him morning and hugged him.

'I slept peacefully. Hope you had a good sleep too?' I asked.

'Yea I did. You want some coffee.'

'No listen to me. I want something from you,' I said.

'What?'

'Promise me we would be together always. Promise me that let whatever happens, we would never leave each other, and promise me you would always love the way you love me now.'

'Baby I promise I will never leave you alone and love you till my last breath.'

'I love you.'

I hurriedly got ready and took a cab from the resort and left lest I would be late for office. Before leaving I promised Tob to see him soon.

I went to my cube, checked my mails and started working. I had deadlines to follow, releases to go but I was still not able to concentrate. I wasn't able to figure out what it was, was it Bee's new relationship that I was scared of or was it my new found relationship with Tob. I was confused.

Missing someone had never been my cup of tea; I don't know why I kept missing Tob. I tried a lot to get him off my mind but bad day it was. That was not something on which I had a control, I did nothing about it; thought of calling him up once I take a break. I tried working for a while but I wasn't able to concentrate. For some reason I was very restless, and I thought speaking to him would make me feel better.

So I finally locked my system and walked up to the cafeteria to call up Tob.

The phone kept ringing and as usual no one responded. I tried calling him again and again but no luck. Ok, he might me busy, he would call me when he is free. But now I should take a coffee, go back and work. I prepared coffee for me, I thought I could work but I wasn't able to do that too. I stood there for half an hour sipping the coffee that got cold till I was very exhausted, and then went back to my laptop feeling nostalgic.

Why the hell did I have to fall for him?

No. How the hell did I even fall for someone? This is ridiculous Nora; I kept saying to myself looking at my phone once in a while expecting a call. I was returning from office in the evening when I received a call from Tob.

'Honey I am so sorry, I was at work, the phone was on silent mode and I never realized you called.'

'It's ok. Don't bother. Hope your day was fine. So what plans for the evening?'

'Nothing much. Will have to speak to few artists in the evening. Need to arrange the DJ or a popular band. Rest seems to be under control. Their event associate is helping me out with other stuffs. What about you? How did your day go?' he asked.

'Yes. It was good. Long day,' I replied.

'So when do you see me?'

'Soon. May be on Thursday. I leave for Bees wedding on Friday.'

'Cool. Let me know when you come. Will cancel other plans.'

I went to bed a little tensed and I dreamt a horrible dream. I saw the end of my relation with Tob. I was ditched and left alone to fend for myself. I started weeping and finally I was struggling with my breath. I could feel drops of sweat coming down from my forehead. When a tear drop entered one of my eyes I woke up.

Yes, that was a dream. And it was a big relief to realize that it was a dream.

I quickly called up Tob and he picked up my call this time. We talked for a few minutes and hanged up because it was a working day and I had to get myself ready for office.

That was a bad and busy day. Nothing went right except the consecutive meetings. Or maybe I was just low which made me feel worse.

I had two more days to leave for Bees wedding so I planned to take a day off and spend some time with Tob. I called him up to say that I would drop in at the resort in the next evening but as usual he didn't pick up the call. I didn't have a choice but to wait for him to call. Everything seemed to be very empty for a moment. There were no phone calls, no noise, nothing happened and I felt lonely.

Being restless I texted Bee.

- Bee, you there.

I waited for a while but there was no response.

She would probably be busy with the pre marriage rituals. It's just 3 days to go so there would be lots of thing to be done.

I thought I would call Angela. But yes that was a bad day. She didn't pick up the call either. Ok, she might be busy with her "would be"…

Finally, I packed my clothes and other necessary items. I packed enough so that I could go directly to the airport from the resort. Next day I booked a cab that would come after office and take me to the resort. I didn't inform Tob of my visit that day as I thought of reaching him directly and giving him a surprise.

The day was a busy one. I had applied for a day off for Bees wedding but that day was the day for sprint planning so I had to do it all beforehand. The meetings took almost half of my day. So, the second half was all about work and mails. I had two more mails to reply when I received a call from the cab driver.

Mam, I reached your office.

'Give me 10 minutes sir, I'll be there.'

After sending the replies, I rushed out. The traffic was as usual very heavy and I was sure I would be late. Well it was better to be late rather than waiting for Tob, he might be off to the site, and I remembered he said that he usually visited the event site every evening.

We were stuck somewhere in the traffic when I saw a lady looking like Bee; her toe finger was hurt when a bike hit her while crossing the road. Her finger was bleeding and she realized it once she reached the other side. Looking at her I felt like calling up Bee but as there was a lot of noise around, I texted her.

- What's up?

- Just saw a lady who reminded me of you.

I was expecting her to reply within seconds but I didn't get any response.

I put my mobile back. She would call me once she sees my text.

Waiting by the heavy traffic for the vehicle to move was tiring and at the same time boring. Having no much option to get rid of the boredom, I tried to talk to the driver.

'Sir, how much time would it take to reach the resort,' I asked the driver.

'Two hours madam.'

He uttered those three words with hesitation and kept mum. That was expected. Moreover he might not be good at conversation. I tried working it out from my side.

'So where are you from?'

'I am from a village near Bellary. But I stay her in Sivaji Nagar.'

'Oh that's great. So you got your family here?'

'Yes my wife and a daughter "Amreen".'

'Wow. She must be beautiful. I was excited to hear him speaking.'

'Yes. She is. I have her picture. You want to see her?' he asked.

'Sure. I would love to.'

He reached for his wallet that was in the dashboard and showed me a passport photo of his daughter. She wasn't that fair but she was beautiful.

'Wow. She is amazing. How old is she?'

'She is 6 yrs. old.'

'Aww...she is beautiful. And I returned him his photo. Tell me about your place and I am sorry I didn't get your name.'

'Madam I am Abdul.' My place is somewhere towards north of Karnataka. It is a village near Bellary, some 30 minutes journey by bus. Beautiful place, but our village is a small one, not so developed.'

Abdul gradually felt comfortable speaking to me which was a kind of a relief and I reached resort within 2 hours that to without being exhausted.

That was already 9p.m. when we reached. I paid him and got off the cab.

'Thanks Abdul. It was nice meeting you. See you then.'

'Madam, you can keep my card. I don't usually pick personal customers, just work for the travel agency, but when I am free I do. So give me a call if you need a cab anytime. I would come or arrange one for you.' And he handed me over a card with his number.

'Thank you Abdul. Hope to see you again.'

'Thank you Madam. Bye.'

I walked towards the resort putting his card in my hand bag. Tob's room was on the 4th floor and the lift just went up. I was excited; I wasn't able to wait for the lift to come down so I took the stairs. I was tired but didn't feel the exhaustion till I reached his room. I was drenched with sweat all over. I knocked at his door and waited with expectation and excitement. I thought that he would be surprised to see me and possibly would hug me. But someone else opened the door for me. What I saw was a girl wearing his shirt, only the shirt, holding a glass of red "whatever" drink and leaning on the door. Well she was beautiful.

'Hey,' she said with arrogance and rudeness stamped on it.

At first I was bewildered and then a bit rattled. I came without informing Tob only to surprise him but I had no idea that greatest surprise of my life was waiting for me. I tried to collect myself in order to respond but my voice choked and nothing came out. It took a while for the truth to sink in. Then I was shocked, stupefied and I kept looking at her as if she were a strange animal from another planet. Tob came out in a minute, he was shirtless. He was surprised to see me there. I knew he would have never expected me to be there, but this wasn't even what I expected too.

'Nora, listen,' he said coming closer to me after the girl walked inside the room without reacting.

I was somewhat restrained till then but when I saw him, I became so furious that I was unable to react. I simply looked at him with tears in my eyes. He tried to assuage my feelings by explaining the circumstances under which the girl happened to be there. He thought he could convince me by giving some trivial excuse. But I was not to be.

I kept looking at him for a while, thinking what I should say and found no words to describe what I was thinking. I appeared really stupid when I smiled, turned around and walked away.

'Nora, stop. Please don't go. Please. I love you.'

'Tob, stop there, if you ever loved me...and you would never follow me. I said without looking back and ran down the stairs towards the parking.

Chapter 19

I ran and ran through parking field to find a way out till I got knocked by a stone and fell down crying out loud. It was dark and no one was there or at least I couldn't be seen because of the darkness. I kept lying there for a while.

'Where should I go? Should I call up Bee? No she is out of station. Harry? He or even any cab would take time to reach here and this place is suffocating for me.'

'OH, Abdul, I remember.'

I took his card out, dialed his number.

'Abdul, could you come back to the resort to pick me up please. The person I had to meet has left.'

'Ok madam, I am coming in 15 minutes,' he said.

I got up and waited wondering what had just happened till the cab reached. I gathered myself and got into cab wiping my tears off my eyes.

'We go back to Whitefield Abdul,' I said.

'Sure madam.'

I leaned back and closed my eyes. I was deeply hurt. Betrayed, ditched and kicked on my back. My pride was crushed, self-esteem gone. I was terribly angry with myself. It was foolish of me to trust a man whom I had met only twice or thrice. My acquaintance with him was too short a period to expect something else, I reasoned. I should not feel hurt. There were tears still running from my eyes and I never realized when I dozed off. Abdul woke me up.

'Madam, madam, we would be reaching Whitefield in a while. Where shall I drop you.'

'Oh yes, sorry I slept.'

That's fine. No issues. Your mobile was ringing but you looked so tired that I didn't feel like waking you up, replied Abdul.

I gave him my address and he took me there. I paid him the fare and walked listlessly to my room. I wasn't drunk but I felt as if I was under the intoxication of some wine. Maybe whatever had happened was too much to take. I opened my door, got in locking it from inside, threw my bags and jumped into my bed and lay on my back looking at the ceiling. The entire picture of what happened to me during the past few days- the unfortunate journey to Goa, the fateful meeting with Tob, a short-lived relationship and its disastrous end- flashed in my mind. I pulled my pillow and wept bitterly for may be an hour and then I slept. Believe me, crying out loud works for me.

Next day, I woke up by a phone call from Dad. Never sure how it happened every time that dad somehow always called me up when I was broken, without even knowing about it.

'Good morning. Wake up for breakfast. It's late,' he said.

'Dad, speak to me for a while. I want to talk to you.'

The last night episode made my morning dull, hazy and suffocating. Speaking to dad would perhaps make me feel better. It is my dad who comes to my rescue whenever I am in trouble. His calm and composed voice would invariably soothe my turbulent mood. But that day was different. He didn't know about my relation with Tob, nor did I ever dare to tell him about it. What would I say to him? I could neither tell him the truth nor could he suggest me anything without being aware of the fact. But that didn't matter. At that moment I would have taken every single word of him as an inspiration.

'Dad, tell me a story. Please.' I knew that it was stupidity on the part of a matured, working girl to request her dad to tell her a story. It sounded funny.

'Now? Get up, and have your breakfast first,' he said.

'Dad, Please. I don't feel good.'

Hmmm. He thought for a while and then started narrating the story of KingLear, one of the great Shakespearean tragedies. The presentation and the choice of words were so lively that I was spellbound. I silently listened to him with all my attention for more than half an hour and then I felt a drop of tear running down my cheek. I felt relatively calm to think of something else.

Next day was my flight and I had my stuffs packed already. So I wasn't left with anything much to do. I checked my mobile. I was expecting a call from Tob; at least a text of apology, but there was nothing. I thought of calling up Bee and speak to her for a while. I found her mobile switched off and there was no response from her local number. I had no other option but to call her mother. She responded but seemed restless.

'Hey Mimi, this is Nora here. Can I speak to Bee?'

'No, I afraid you cannot.' She said and started weeping.

'What happened to you Mimi? Is everything fine?'

'No. Nothing is fine. She isn't here. She has left.'

She cried loudly and that was getting into my nerves. I tried to persuade her to calm down but my efforts went in vain.

'Please tell me Mimi what happened,' I requested her.

'Nora, honey, tomorrow is her wedding and she isn't anywhere here. She might have fled sometime last night or very early this morning leaving a note behind.

"I am not happy with whatever is happening, neither am I able to convince myself to take everything in my stride. I tried hard but I think I cannot take this anymore. I know this step of mine would offend you all and you would be mad at my selfishness for a while but believe me I have done this for my future, you will realize it later. Love, Bee."

'What? How the hell could she do this? If this is what she wanted then she would have done it earlier. Why now when there is not even a day to go. Jesus, this lady is impossible. Mimi, have any idea where could she have gone?'

'No beta, we have no idea. We are trying to contact her but her mobile is switched off. Nora, can you please help searching for her. Talk to her friends and enquire if she reached out to anyone or if they know anything about this girl. I would be very thankful to you.'

'Common, Mimi. You don't need to say this. Let me talk to my friends and see if she is in touch with them. And I will give you a call soon. Mimi, please don't worry, everything's gona be fine.'

I forgot my own pain I remembered the lines- 'when the greater wound afflict the mind, the lesser ones are scarcely felt.' This was second shock I received during the last few hours. I sat down and it took me a while to be normal and I tried to figure out why did she do such a foolish thing and where would she be gone? But why didn't she text me, she could have at least texted me. Whom would she have reached out to then, Harry? Angela?

I talked to them to check if Bee was in touch with them. But I got a negative reply.

Who else then?

I kept on thinking harder. Where the hell is she? It is not possible for her to leave the country at such a short time. She must be somewhere here in Bangalore or with some acquaintance. Where would I go if the same situation arose in my life? I kept questioning myself. I called her roomie, she wasn't there too. What next? I didn't know. The only thing that I was sure about was that I would not be going anywhere that day. After trying out several calls, I was exhausted. I threw my phone on the bed and went straight to take a shower

Chapter 20

That was post lunch when I contacted a few more common friends to check if they had any idea. No luck. I tried calling on Bee's personal number again. "Beep Beep Beep, the number you are trying to reach is currently switched off. Please try after sometime". Goodness this is not working out and I felt a bit frustrated. Suddenly I heard the recorded voice of a woman in 'Marathi' before my phone was disconnected. Then I shouted, "Nora, I think you know where she is.'

I opened my laptop quickly, cancelled the tickets for Bees wedding and booked a ticket to Goa and a cab to the airport for the next day.

I packed two pair of clothes, the mobile charger, my wallet, toothbrush and my first aid box. That was all I required. If I found Bee I would try to convince her to return at least to her work place.

That was a restless night and I was in a state of confusion. I could clearly see the damage she had done to her and to her family. It was nothing less than self-destruction. But I failed to understand her attitude in regard to arranged marriages. Though I tried hard, I wasn't able to sleep. So, finally I got up from my bed very early in the morning and got ready to go.

I reached Dabolim airport by 9 in the morning and rushed for a taxi to take me to Arambol. It was my assumption that she might be there at Arambol. I wasn't even sure if I would find her there or not, but still that was worth a try.

It was sunny outside and the air conditioner lulled me into sleep in the cab. I slept for nearly two hours and woke up when we reached the place. I paid the fare and walked towards the beach with my bag pack hanging by my shoulders. Immediately I began searching for Bee first in the shops and then in the café we visited last time. Thereafter I went to Buddha Palace expecting to find her. But she was not to be found anywhere. I was too tired to walk; so, I sat at a table in despair. A waiter noticed me and asked if I needed anything.' Get me a bottle of water, please.' The waiter returned with a bottle of cold water. I thanked him and drank some water. I thought it futile to search her in Goa. I was about to get up when I noticed a shadow in front of me. I could not believe my eyes when I saw Bee standing there.

"How did you know I am here," she asked and flung herself on me to hug me.

She was dressed as if she was on a holiday-a colorful jumpsuit, with a pair of aviator glasses and a flower tucked on her hair.

'What the hell is wrong with you? Are you out of your senses? You ran away a day before your wedding and looks like you are enjoying your holiday here when everyone else over there is worried about you. How can you be so insensitive to your parents?'

'Nora, cool down.' She said taking a seat, and asked me to do the same.

'I know what I am doing. I don't say I am correct, I might be wrong, very wrong but sometimes it's about one's choices. As you said, if I regret for what I did today I can convince myself saying, it was my choice.

And I was doing it for what? My parents happiness right, don't worry I would make them happy. There are other ways to make them happy.'

'Bee, I understand your point but everyone is worried, they don't even know where you are. You would have at least told someone about it.'

'Dad knows about it. He knows where I am. I spoke to him a day before. Mom doesn't, but I am sure he has his own ways to make her understand. So chill, everything is under control. This is not the end of the world.'

I kept looking at her with surprise while she leaned back on her chair looking at the rustling waves and started humming.

* *